THE BANISHED HIGHLANDER

Copyright © 2019 by Keira Montclair

Printed in the USA.

Cover Design and Interior Format

THE BANISHED HIGHLANDER

KEIRA MONTCLAIR

PROLOGUE

13th century, the Highlands of Scotland

JULIANA CLAVELLE BOLTED UP IN her bed, surprised to see her older sister, Joan, was not asleep next to her. Something had awakened her. She held her breath and listened, so afraid of the dark that a small whimper came from deep within her belly. She didn't scream because Papa was always telling her to be a big lass. Now that she was eight winters, she would be.

But her hands clenched around her beloved stuffed bunny when she heard her sire bellowing in the next chamber. "You will marry him!"

Juliana crept over to the door, her bunny squeezed tightly against her chest, her fingers brushing its worn ears lovingly.

Joan sobbed. "Please, Papa. Do not force me to marry him. I hate him."

Juliana feared the inevitable had happened. Her mother had always warned her that Joan, who had just turned eight and ten, would marry one day and leave, but she hadn't wished to believe her.

"He's of noble blood, I could not find you a better marriage. He's willing to pay good coin for you. You may not like him now, but you'll learn to care for him."

Her mother's voice carried through the drafty wooden door. "Richard," she said softly, placatingly, "he does not seem to be a nice man. I don't wish to send her to someone who would beat her."

"He'll treat her right. I'll be sure of it. You'll marry him, Joan, and you'll stop this nonsense." Their sire sounded more and more English as he continued to rail on her sister. Although their mother was Scottish, and their family had lived near the Lowlands of Scotland for all of Juliana's life, their sire was always praising the English ways.

"Who taught you to be so defiant? Girls should be quiet and obedient, or shall I thrash you until you understand?"

Juliana swore to herself that she'd be quiet and obedient from that day forward so her father wouldn't speak to her in such a manner.

And yet, she could tell Joan had no intention to do as their father bid.

"I'll run away before I marry him," her sister said, her tone fierce. "You'll see."

"And where will you go?"

"To Lochluin Abbey. I'll take my vows."

CHAPTER ONE

—◆—

Twelve years later

JULIANA REINED IN HER HORSE as her guards came to a sudden stop.

They were less than two hours away from Lochluin Abbey, or so the guards had just announced before stopping in the middle of a meadow. It was clear one of the men had heard something.

All six of them were on alert, their gazes scanning the forest surrounding the meadow. The budding of the trees hampered their view, although not much.

"We're nearly on Cameron land," the leader said. "Reivers don't travel here. You must have heard boars in the bushes." Juliana didn't see anything out of sorts. The guards moved forward slowly, finally making it to a small glen, when something off to the side caught her attention. A moment later, several horses charged toward them.

Juliana screamed, her heart pounding with fear as the marauders approached. They looked so fierce and angry, and worst of all, they were staring straight at her.

The closer they came, the more frightened she became, her gentle mare now rearing from the vibrations in the ground. "Winnie, calm down!" She tried to guide her dear horse away from the attackers, but the animal frantically jerked in different directions.

Juliana couldn't control her.

The guards her sire had hired surrounded her, doing their best to protect her from danger.

"I want her," one reiver shouted. "I need that coin he offered. Hand her over."

He pointed straight at her. *At her!*

Who would offer coin for her? She had little knowledge of men and the outside world, having been protected by her sire. They lived not far from her mother's clan, Clan Culloch, but they rarely visited. Her sire insisted they stay home. She'd never traveled alone before. Never seen a real fight. And now her worst nightmare was unfolding around her.

Her guards ignored the man and continued to fight, the clang of sword against sword ripping through the air. She watched in horror as three of her guards fell down in bloody heaps.

She gripped Winnie's reins so tightly she feared she'd hurt her dear horse. Forcing herself to ease her grip on them, she tried to calm the mare by patting her with one hand as she steered her closer to the remaining guards. Three men weren't enough to surround her, though, and one of the reivers soon broke past them. He got close enough to snake an arm around her waist and yanked her off her horse.

"Too bad, men, but I have her. I'll get the coin for her!" The tattered plaid he wore was so dirty it was unrecognizable. Long brown hair that hadn't been combed in a fortnight fell past his shoulders. His grizzled beard was full of crumbs, but that didn't bother her nearly as much as the crazed look in his eyes.

She screamed just as a few horses barreled into the meadow. The man in front wore a red and green plaid, while the others were red and blue. It was obvious that these were real warriors, stronger and better trained than the men-for-hire protecting her. They cut down her attackers in a matter of minutes, and her kidnapper, deciding he was outmatched, attempted to gallop away, heading toward a ravine. The man in front, dressed in the red-and-green plaid, rode hard in pursuit, bellowing.

She bit her attacker's arm through his tunic, hard enough to hurt, but his slap didn't bother her half so much as the horrible taste. The man with the long dark hair came abreast of them, and in one fluid moved yanked her attacker from his horse and stuck a blade in him. Bright red blood pulsated out of the man's body, shocking her, although she'd seen plenty of blood these last few minutes.

Grabbing the reins of the horse, she slowed the beast now frothing at the mouth, and turned him around to face this new group of men. Had they come to save her, or was this another group of reivers?

Her head spun at the realization that the men her father hired were all dead or incapacitated. Some found their way back to their horses while others still sat on the ground, stunned. The violent attack had taken place in a matter of minutes.

She was as stunned as they were.

One of the men in the new group instructed his men to assist her guards, pointing in the direction he wanted them taken, the word "healer" jumping out at her.

She hoped that's where they'd be taken.

She hadn't expected such a bleak outcome. Forcing her gaze up and away from the injured, she closed her eyes to gather strength, anything to banish the blood and gore from her mind. Another man, a bit older, rode up beside the one who had saved her. "Who are you, lass?" he asked, "and where are you headed? I'm Aedan Cameron, chieftain of Clan Cameron. We'll not hurt you."

She glanced from one face to the other, although she couldn't see either of them clearly because her eyes were brimming with tears. Clan Cameron. The head guard, who now lay dead, had just said they were safe because they were on Cameron land, hadn't he?

Clearly, he had been mistaken in that assumption.

The one who'd saved her from her attacker moved closer. "Lass, 'tis all right. We'll get you to where you were headed. Where were you going?"

"Lochluin Abbey." Her voice cracked, but she managed the words. These men wouldn't hurt her, her gut told her.

"Good," the chieftain said. "We're not far from there. We'd be happy to escort you the rest of the way. Would you prefer to ride that horse or the one you were riding? My brother has rounded up the horses back in the meadow."

"My horse, please. The chestnut color with the white mane. She was a gift from my sire."

The Cameron leaned over to take the reins of the fallen reiver's horse. "Who is your sire?" he asked as he began to lead her back. The other man, the one who'd saved her, rode with them.

"Richard Clavelle. He's English, but my mama is Scottish." How she wished she could stop the trembling in her hands.

"You're doing fine. We'll stay with you until you've arrived at the abbey. And why are you going to Lochluin?"

"My sister is a nun. She is often at Stonecroft Abbey, but she is to be at Lochluin for the next two moons. I'm to visit with her, decide if I wish to take my vows." The horses clattered over the rocky ground, and it was all Juliana could do to hang on through her shock. When they returned to the meadow, she saw the remaining two men from the group of warriors. They'd collected the horses of the fallen and her mare.

"Which one is yours?" her rescuer asked. "This one?" He pointed to Winnie.

"Aye, my thanks." Tears misted her eyes because she was so happy to see her dearest pet. She'd lost her mother a while ago, her sister was a nun, but dear Winnie was always by her side.

She couldn't lose her.

Her rescuer went to retrieve the horse, but he didn't act quickly enough. One of the men who'd collected the horses dismounted and led her mare over. As if she weighed no more than a feather, he lifted her down from the reiver's horse and helped her onto her mount. She was struck by the color of his hair, a dark deep red, and the kindness in his eyes. His hands were rough from the lists, yet they were strangely gentle, too.

Shock still rolled through her, but she managed to clear her head enough to say, "I don't know any of you, but my thanks to you all." Much as she wished, she couldn't stop her hand from rubbing the fur on her horse's back.

"Ruari Cameron, brother to the chieftain," the red-haired man said with a small smile.

"Padraig Grant," her rescuer said. "Cousin."

"Neil, second-in-command of Clan Cameron," said the fourth man, the oldest in the group. "What's your name, lass?"

"I'm Juliana Clavelle."

"Pleased to meet you, my lady," Ruari said, his gaze boring into hers.

A fluttering deep inside her belly spread a wave of heat through her, something she'd never experienced before.

Ruari Cameron was an uncommonly handsome man.

———◆———

Ruari was ready to spew fire across the glen. Had he ridden in alongside his brother, he could have saved the lass, but he'd allowed himself to be distracted, and Padraig had beaten him to it.

For years, Ruari had been eager to prove himself to Aedan, but he was beginning to think he was cursed. Surely he'd accomplished far too little for a man of eight and twenty.

But one glance at his companion was enough to distract him from his own problems. The poor lass was clearly shaken. Although the hood she wore concealed most of her face, he saw the shock and horror in her light brown eyes, almost the same shade of her hair. He suspected she'd never seen so much violence before.

After they'd ridden for nearly half an hour, Aedan signaled for them to stop. "Ruari, you and Padraig will escort the lady the rest of the way. Take her directly to the abbey door. Neil and I will inspect the area for more reivers. I'd like to know why these men attacked a group of travelers so close to the abbey. This is most unusual."

"Aye, you can count on me," Ruari said, grateful he could do this one small thing. Mayhap he could offer some words of comfort to the lass. Help her through her hardships.

But as soon as the older men left, Padraig jumped right in with his casual teasing, not allowing Ruari the chance to talk at all. "You wish to take your vows, lass? You're much too pretty to be a nun."

Ruari glanced at her, catching a flash of pink cheeks before she looked at Padraig, who rode on the opposite side of her. She said nothing.

"You know how pretty you are, do you not?" Padraig persisted.

She kept her gaze straight ahead this time, ignoring him.

Padraig didn't stop with his casual entertainment. "Look at all the creatures coming out to admire you. There's a hare staring straight at you, over there is a red squirrel, and I can almost hear that otter over there asking, 'Where is she? I wish to see her…'"

When he still didn't get a reaction from the lass, Padraig shrugged his shoulders and glanced at Ruari. Usually, the lad was able to get a laugh from most anyone.

"Mayhap she'd prefer you to be quiet, Padraig," Ruari drawled. Although he was grateful Padraig, their cousin by marriage, had come to foster with his brother, the lass appeared immune to his charms. Not a surprise given what she'd been through, and her wish to become a nun.

But the lass surprised him. The lightest of giggles came from underneath her hood, and Juliana shifted her head to glance at Ruari before looking at Padraig. "I don't see an otter," she said. "You're telling tales."

Padraig gave her a wide grin, encouraged by the attention, and said, "You missed him. I for certes saw one. Did you not, Ruari?"

"Most surely I did not, you wee fool." And because he wished to please her, he added, "Anyone with eyes would know it was a badger."

"Excuse me, but I beg you not to insult me again, Cameron. I may be a *big* fool, but I'm surely not a wee one. And I do have two eyes in my head."

She laughed again, the sound surprisingly musical, and pulled her hood back enough for them to see more of her face. "I don't mind if he wishes to talk," she said, "but I don't know either of you well enough to converse. Papa tells me I should keep quiet around strangers."

Ruari quirked his brow at the lass, trying to conceal his sudden dislike for her sire. "He does? I don't know many lasses who are quiet. I have two nieces and they never stop chattering."

Padraig, serious for a change, asked, "Tell me true. Do you really wish to become a nun?"

She glanced at him and tipped her head. "I'm not sure. I'll be here for a fortnight. I'll know better by the end of my journey."

"But why would you choose to become a nun?" Padraig asked, not taking his gaze from her. "I never understood it."

"To serve our Lord."

That left Padraig speechless, something that rarely happened. But their opportunity to continue their conversation came to an end since they'd arrived at the gates of the abbey. Ruari did manage to shove Padraig out of the way so he could help Juliana down from her horse.

She didn't weigh any more than his nephew Brin, who was only ten summers.

She blushed as he set her feet on the ground, but he said nothing, not wishing to embarrass her further.

Padraig's words must have caught up with him, for he said, "Ruari, must you be so rough on the lass? She nearly fell to her knees." He had a teasing glint in his eyes, something that had become quite familiar in the months he'd spent on Cameron land.

Juliana giggled again, covering her mouth. "Nay, I did not, but I believe you know that, my lord."

Padraig jumped off his horse and spun around in a circle. "My lord? Who are you speaking to?"

Her finger pointed to him and he guffawed. "Lass, call me Padraig. I'm only six and ten, and for certes no lord. A big fool, a beast, or a bastard as my cousin often calls me, but no lord. Your Lord is inside the abbey there."

Juliana exploded into laughter, hiding her face in her hands in a futile attempt to hide her giggles. This time Ruari felt a pulse of gratitude—the lad had made her forget her troubles, if only for a moment—and he couldn't help but smile. It was a lovely laugh, and he wished to hear it often.

He reached up for her saddlebag, then ushered her toward the front entrance of the abbey. Although Padraig took a step forward as if to join them, Ruari shook his head. "Stay put." He gave his cousin a harsh look to let him know he meant it.

When they stepped into the abbey, Juliana finally dropped the hood of her mantle, her gaze taking in the passageway and the chamber meant for receiving guests. Her eyes looked huge, and it struck him that the lass had been through quite a lot in a short period of time. She had to feel overwhelmed by the experience.

A moment later, the abbess, Mother Mathilda, stepped into the small space to greet them.

"Greetings to you, Mother Matilda," he said.

"Master Cameron. Who have you brought me this day? Is this Sister Joan's sister, Juliana?"

"Aye, and here are her things." He set the saddlebag down on the stone floor. Juliana still had not said anything, so he explained, "Lady Juliana's guards were attacked by reivers. She's a wee bit upset."

"Didn't I just hear her laughing?" Mother Matilda asked, her gaze searching both faces.

Ruari could not help but smile at that, proving something he'd always known. The abbess didn't miss much. "Aye, my cousin Padraig was spreading his usual merriment, but I do wish for you to know 'twas a trying and exhausting journey for the young lass." His hand went to the small of her back of its own will.

"I see. Aye, I am familiar with Padraig's sense of humor. He can be a delight or quite exhausting. Reivers, you say?" the abbess asked. "Will our torment never stop?" She shook her head and folded her arms in front of her. Before anything else could be said, a nun he'd never met flew down the hall and swept Juliana into an embrace. Their eyes were the same unusual shade of light brown, almost gold.

"I've been waiting for you all day! I've missed you so," Sister Joan said, then stepped back to assess her. "You're upset. What happened?"

"They were attacked by reivers," Ruari said, taking a step forward. "I'm from Clan Cameron. We took care of the men who did it, but we didn't arrive soon enough to save all of her guards. Some are dead, others injured. The injured are being escorted to Mistress Jennie. It was too late for some, and for that, I sincerely apologize."

Juliana turned her face toward Ruari, tears misting her gaze as if the attack had only just caught up to her.

He'd have to thank Padraig for doing such a fine job of distracting her on the ride to the abbey.

Staring up at him, she said, "My thanks to you for all your assistance, but I'd like to rest now. Joan," she said, turning to the nun. "Please take me to your chamber."

Ruari took a final glance at Juliana, suddenly struck by her beauty, as if a branch had fallen on his head to make him pay attention. He'd noticed she was pretty, but he'd been wrong.

Juliana Clavelle was the loveliest lass he'd ever seen.

CHAPTER TWO

RUARI TOOK HIS LEAVE, BUT before he could mount his horse, he heard soft steps running toward him from the abbey. Juliana. She was almost upon him when he turned to see her flushed and breathless.

"My lady, did you forget something?" he asked.

"Nay," she said, her gaze traveling to Padraig before darting back to him. She stared at him for a long moment without saying anything.

He didn't know how to react to that, so he said nothing, giving her the time she needed.

"Well, aye. I forgot to properly thank both of you. I know we were jesting along the way, but I wish to be verra serious when I tell you how much I appreciate that you both came to my assistance when I desperately needed it. I'm not often away from home." She glanced back at Padraig, although her gaze once again landed on Ruari. "When I think about what could have happened…"

"'Twas our duty and our pleasure, lass," Ruari said, his voice coming out in a husky tone he hadn't expected.

Ruari's gaze fell on her lips. On the exact spot where her teeth bit the bottom lip enough to plump it out a bit more than it was naturally. Pink and desirable, begging to be kissed. Porcelain skin with a slight dotting of freckles decorated the bridge of her petite nose. She lifted her chin a notch, and the smooth skin of her neck beckoned him.

He mentally shook himself, forcing his gaze back to her

face. What the hell was wrong with him?

Her hand settled on his forearm, and it was as if she branded him with a searing heat. "I am extremely grateful to both of you."

She spun on her heel and hurried back inside, leaving Ruari at a loss for words.

"What's wrong?" Padraig asked.

"Naught, I..."

"What?"

He mounted his horse in one quick movement. "I didn't notice her beauty until she dropped her hood. The lass is stunning."

"Then mayhap you should convince her not to take her vows," Padraig said with a wink. "A few sweet words could take you verra far."

"Sweet words are not one of my finer attributes. Besides, once was enough for me. I'll not marry again."

"Nay, don't say that. Never is a long time, cousin."

Ruari had married the prettiest lass in the clan. They hadn't married for love, but he'd been fond of Doirin. Still, the marriage had always felt...incomplete. Their affection had never blossomed into anything more powerful, and they'd never had children. They'd argued about that, bitterly, right before the accident that had claimed her life. He'd asked her to consult with Jennie about her inability to carry, but she'd refused. Both of them had raised their voices, and she'd stormed off to go riding.

Once Ruari's anger had passed, he went after her, knowing how she loved to push her horse. To his surprise, he'd found Neil at her side, tending her dead body, her horse not far away with a sprained leg. Doirin's neck had broken from a fall.

Three years had passed, but he still thought of it each and every day. He'd failed Doirin, and in his heart, he didn't believe he deserved another chance.

"Aye," he said softly, "forever is a long time, but I'll not do it."

"You were at my cousins' wedding not long ago. You must have seen how joyful they were. Don't you wish for the same?" The double wedding, held at Lochluin Abbey, had been a huge event, attended by everyone in the clan. There was no denying the two couples had looked deliriously happy, but he didn't trust his own judgment when it came to lasses.

"I did. No more. 'Tis not for me." Nay, he'd decided his purpose was to be of service to his brother and the clan. Nothing and no one would sway him.

———————

Juliana flopped onto the bed in the chamber she was to share with her dear sister. "'Twas awful, Joan. I was so frightened. If the Cameron men hadn't come along, those brutes would have carried me away. I'd be better off marrying the man Papa favors. I nearly died."

"I'm so glad I found out about this possible betrothal. I made him promise long ago that he would send you to the abbey for a proper visit before you marry. I had to send a messenger to remind him of that, or he would have made you marry this man right away." Joan crossed her arms in front of her, her expression fierce. "Now, who does he wish for you to marry?"

"You wish to approve of my husband? But I thought you wanted me to become a nun like you so we could always be together?"

Joan sat down next to her and clasped her hands. "I *do* wish you would choose the nunnery, but 'tis a decision for you to make on your own. I cannot make it for you, and neither can Papa. He would respect your choice if you insisted on becoming a novice. But I'm happy you're here regardless of what you wish to do. I can help you understand the truth about marriage. Did Mama tell you about the expectations a husband has for his wife?"

Juliana pursed her lips, moving them from one side to the other. "You mean that lasses must be quiet and obedient?"

"Nay, not that, though 'tis exactly what most men expect. The marriage bed. Did she not explain it to you after you started your monthly courses? I know it has been two years since she was with us, but I thought she would have told you long ago."

Juliana scowled because she felt at a complete loss. Her mother had told her nothing about what to expect of marriage. While she'd heard talk among serving maids and stable lads, she'd never truly understood it. "Nay, what of it? Are there special linens or something? Would I not just sleep in my own chamber next to my husband?"

Joan groaned loudly enough to make her feel foolish. She'd clearly gotten it all wrong.

"Joan, I've heard of the sweating and grunting and all that from the serving maids, but married couples don't do that, do they? I thought they were teasing me because of the way animals mate in the stables…" A moment of silence hung between them. "But." A few things suddenly started to make sense to her, something she hadn't taken the time to think about before. "It truly happens that way?"

"Oh my, 'tis exactly as I feared. I have much to teach you, but we'll worry about that another day." Joan stood and paced, working her fingers across her lips as she thought. "I must warn you about the realities of being wed. You should be aware of that before you make your decision."

That sounded ominous, and Juliana wasn't sure she could stomach it just now, not when she hadn't eaten anything for hours. "Joan, I'm hungry. Must we wait until the last meal of the day? Have you some broth or something? Then I'd like to rest a bit. 'Twas a most exhausting journey."

Guilt and worry crossed her sister's face. "You poor thing! Of course, you must be hungry. And to think, you were attacked by reivers. I would have been hysterical by now. Allow me to run to the kitchens and I'll return straight away. Can you busy yourself until then? I promise to return quickly. There must be bread and cheese at the verra least." Her sister turned back a full three times before she headed to the door.

"Aye, I can find something to do. I'll unpack a few things while you're gone."

"Aye, aye." She came back to give her a quick hug. "My apologies for not being more considerate about the situation. I'm sure you are upset and tired. Please put your things in that chest, and the small side table is for your notions." Joan skittered away, but not before she made one final comment. "Juliana, I'm so pleased you are here with me. Please don't regret your journey, as troublesome as it was. We need this time together. Both of us do."

She disappeared so quickly that Juliana had no time to reply, but she decided Joan was correct. They *did* deserve time together. She vowed not to focus on the horrible circumstances of the journey.

She would focus on her sister.

Juliana sat staring at the door. Their sire had never forgiven Joan for running off to the convent rather than marrying the husband he favored, and Joan had never forgiven him for leaving her with no choice. Although Father claimed he wasn't to blame for their infrequent visits with Joan, Juliana wasn't sure what to believe. She and her sister hadn't seen each other since their mother's funeral, two years ago. There was a distance between them she did not like. One she hoped would ease over the course of this visit.

Her mind drifted to the man with the dark-red hair— Ruari Cameron. She'd thought him handsome from the start, but when she'd stepped close to him, actually peered into his warm brown eyes, her belly had done an odd flip-flop.

The man had a chiseled jaw that begged to be touched. But what she'd liked most about him was his smile. Wide and genuine, it had made something inside her happy to behold it. How she wished she could get to know him better. Make him smile.

Later, when she'd touched his arm, it had felt like something was passing between them. Almost as if their souls had met before, and they were happy to see each other again.

She hadn't felt the same about the other guard, Padraig. He was quite a jester, but he didn't call to her soul the way Ruari did.

She would never forget Ruari Cameron, even if they never met again.

Which was likely, given she was to spend the next fortnight in the abbey. Heaving a sigh, she rose to her feet. After she finished moving her clothing from her bag into the chest, she took out her needlework and began to work.

Needlework calmed her, so she was often working on one project or another. She'd made pillow covers and small wall decorations, but this was her most ambitious project ever.

She'd had a vision of a field full of purple flowers, the scent of lavender heady as she ran through it. This was her first attempt at bringing a true natural setting to her work. If it came out well, she wished to make a wall hanging of it, perhaps for Joan, or she could keep it and take it with her to her next home, whether she married or took her vows.

Something told her that her vision of the flowers was important. That she needed to convey the beauty in her mind onto the cloth. In her heart, she knew there was a reason for it, yet she had no idea what it might be. And somehow she knew it was missing something, but she couldn't figure out what.

It would come to her when it was needed.

CHAPTER THREE

THE NEXT MORN, RUARI AND Padraig were practicing their sword work on their own, heaving and sweating without any attention for their surroundings, when Neil approached the courtyard. He'd been Aedan's second-in-command for many years—a job Ruari had always wanted.

Neil knew, of course, and he loved to flaunt his power around Ruari. Although the man had never liked him, he'd become much nastier after Doirin's accident. He'd always placed the blame squarely on Ruari's shoulders, and a fortnight after her death, he'd even told Ruari he thought Aedan should have banished him from the clan. That sentiment hadn't been repeated, but Ruari had never forgotten it.

The older man chuckled darkly as he walked up to them. "'Tis not your sword skills that need practicing, Ruari. How did your favorite spying tactic work for you with those reivers?"

Ruari said nothing. He would not give the man the satisfaction of speaking. They both knew he'd handled the situation poorly.

"No words of wisdom for me?" Neil pressed. "Did ye congratulate your brother for saving the lass? Your brother and the fine lad you're sparring with were the true heroes of the day."

Ruari said naught, though it was increasingly difficult to

remain quiet.

Padraig spoke up in his defense. "Mayhap he was last, but you were not far ahead of him, Neil. Don't think you should be throwing any stones at him. What kept you? Was it your age?"

Neil huffed and spun on his heel, leaving the two cousins alone.

"My thanks to you, Padraig," Ruari murmured low enough so he could not be overheard.

"The man never stops, does he? Why does your brother insist on keeping him as his second? You're a much harder worker, and everyone knows it. That fool just likes to prance around and give orders. He's past his best years, and you are a much better swordsman."

Ruari found himself in the uncomfortable position of defending a man who looked at him with nothing but contempt. "When he was younger, he was a fine second." He grabbed his waterskin up off the ground, took a few swigs, then tossed it aside.

As if the skin were his brother's head.

He spat not far from the skin, grateful Padraig couldn't read his thoughts. He loved his brother. He respected his brother.

He wished he could earn Aedan's respect in return.

"I cannot believe you would defend him." Padraig took a long look at him, too insightful given his age. "Or is it your brother you defend?"

"My brother," he admitted. "Aedan has much on his hands. Lately, he's needed to defend the abbey as much as our land."

Although the abbey was not directly affiliated with the Camerons, they'd been called upon to assist in its protection many times over the years. It was a duty they all took to heart. The monks there worked tirelessly creating and duplicating the church's finest tomes and documents, while the nuns did God's work in so many ways.

Padraig grunted. "Someday he'll make the right choice." He paced a few circles around Ruari, then picked up his sword, taking a stance opposite him.

Ruari just nodded, going after the lad with renewed vigor.

How could he explain to his cousin that his greatest fear was that Aedan would replace Neil with someone else when the time came?

In fact, it had occurred to him that Aedan could be fostering Padraig in the hopes the young Grant would stay on and become his second someday.

Would his own brother do that to him?

When their sire had taken his last breath, he'd begged Aedan to take over as chieftain. He'd had to beg because Aedan hadn't wanted any part of leading the clan.

Ruari would have been overjoyed to become chief, but the brothers were far apart in age, and he'd only been one and ten at the time.

He gave credit where it was due. Aedan had become a fine chieftain, and he'd ably defended their land and the abbey against multiple marauders and thieves over the years.

If only Ruari could have taken a larger part.

His brother had thought he was too young to help at first, and so he'd spent his time spying on their allies. In doing so, he alone had uncovered a plot to overthrow his brother. The whole clan had shouted his praises for two moons after that, and he'd loved every minute of the glory.

But the glory had dissipated quickly, and no matter how hard he tried, he couldn't duplicate it. Spying had become second nature to him—he was uncommonly good at it—but spying wasn't the answer to every problem. Still, he couldn't shake his habit of taking a covert approach. Sneaking up on people, hiding in the bushes, training his ears to listen to others' conversations became a part of him. His tendency was to collect the full picture before riding in to attack—something that had earned him plenty of taunting from others in the clan. Neil wasn't the only one who thought him a fool.

He took a step back from sparring and finally decided to put the question directly to Padraig. Although young, the lad had good sense. "What is my problem?"

Padraig tossed his weapon to the ground, then wiped the sweat off his brow with his tunic. "Ruari, you're a fine swordsman. You have good sense, but you shouldn't have attempted to ride around the group of reivers yesterday. We knew everything we needed to know to save the lass. Perhaps you should talk to your brother about all of this. Ask him why he hasn't made you his second yet."

Ruari dropped his weapon and reached for the skin of ale, which he'd brought alongside the water. He chugged down some ale, thinking of the ten different conversations he'd had with his brother over the years. "I have. He always gives me the same answer. I don't have the experience."

"Have you asked him why he thinks you struggle to distinguish yourself in battle?"

Ruari nearly spat his drink out.

Padraig smirked and clasped his shoulder. "Think on it. After all Aedan has been through, he should be able to give you great advice. Everyone knows he didn't wish to be chieftain, but he's taken to it like a natural."

"Nay. He thinks he knows what ails me. He always says the same thing. He thinks I'm afraid, but I have no fear that I'm aware of."

"How could you not know your own fears?" Padraig asked.

Oh, he knew them. The fear of failure was his constant companion.

———

Ruari rode his horse out through the gates, needing to be alone. When he was far enough out, he turned his horse toward the mountaintops north of Cameron land.

The Highlands of Scotland beckoned him—the peaks and valleys, the deep green of the forests, the pines and the patches of thick lavender. How he loved this land. He took great pride in both his clan and his country.

If only Ruari could do more to serve them. He'd never wished for Aedan to just hand over the job of the chieftain's second-in-command. He'd wished to earn it.

But it was difficult with Neil's eyes constantly surveying him, waiting for him to make mistakes he could point out to Aedan.

Ruari's late wife, Doirin, had thought him a failure too. She'd pushed him to buy her jewels and gowns. At her bidding, he'd asked Aedan to send them to London to represent Clan Cameron at any royal events—something he'd done to make her happy, not because he actually wished to leave his home. Aedan had told him no.

She had taken it as further proof of his unworthiness.

Although he wasn't proud of it, Ruari had always envied Aedan's happiness with Jennie. Theirs was an ideal marriage, between two people perfectly suited for each other. What would it be like to have that feeling of belonging?

He'd only ever experienced that on Cameron land. He drank in the peacefulness of the day for a moment more, closing his eyes to enjoy the music of the birds, the chittering of the squirrels, the rustling of the leaves, and the wind roaring through the pines.

Bolstered by the sights and sounds of the land he loved, he turned back to the gates. Aedan wasn't the only one he'd avoided of late.

It was time for him to visit his mother.

Something he had come to dread.

Nevertheless, he headed toward the keep to visit her. His mother was no longer able to take care of herself. She stayed in a tower chamber on the first floor because her hips would no longer allow her to go up and down stairs.

Ruari used to take her for short walks out of doors in nice weather, but it had pained him to see her struggle on the slightest of slopes, and so he'd ended their outings. Some days she spoke frequently, other days very little. Her favorite topics were her grandchildren—Brin, Tara, and Riley. She often made comments about wishing Ruari would give her more grandchildren. He ignored them because he knew it could never be, although she seemed convinced it would happen someday.

Once inside the keep, he was surprised to see her seated in front of the hearth, a plaid over her lap. He wondered what could possibly be running through her mind as she stared into the flames.

"Mama? How are you this fine day?" He pulled a chair up next to her. She was one of the only people in the great hall at the moment, although the serving maids bustled in and out as they prepared for the evening meal.

"Ruari, 'tis so nice to see you. I'm well. The fire warms my old bones." She gave him a broad smile, her hand reaching for him.

He took it and held it between his palms, surprised as always by her unnaturally cool skin. "Mama, would you like another plaid? You're so cold."

"I'm fine, lad."

"Mama, I'm not a lad anymore. I'm eight and twenty. Hardly young."

"Don't be silly. You'll always be my laddie."

His mother's gaze returned to the flames, her happiness that he'd joined her clearly evident. Why didn't he come more often?

Because it hurt him to see her this way, and he knew his own mother considered him a failure. Although she'd never come out and said as much, he always heard the message behind her words.

"I see that look in your eyes again, Ruari."

She still gazed at the fire as she said it, so he couldn't

understand how she'd seen anything. But he knew without a doubt he was about to be reminded of his failure. "What look, Mama? I'm just happy to see you."

"That look I've seen so many times over the years. 'Tis not your fault Aedan was our firstborn. It was in the stars. 'Tis no reflection on you or your abilities. 'Twas decided the day he was born that he'd be chieftain someday." She lifted her chin, lost again in memories. "I miss your papa."

"I do, too. I know Aedan was always meant to be chief, Mama. 'Tis as it should be. I can help the clan in other ways."

She patted his hand. "I wish you truly believed that. Have you seen Brin today? My, but he's a talented lad, is he not?"

"Aye, he is."

As if on cue, the door flew open and Brin burst through the door, a handful of spring flowers in his hands. "Here, Grandmama. I found some flowers and brought them for you."

She pulled her hand from Ruari's and clapped her hands together. "Brin, they're beautiful. Many thanks to you."

That was Ruari's cue to leave. He snuck out the door, pausing only to ruffle Brin's hair, and headed out through the gates toward the lists. On the way out, he caught a rustling in the bush off to the side of the path. Wild pigs loved to root in the bushes, so he glanced over to ensure it wasn't a boar ready to charge at him.

A furry head stuck up through the grasses and gave a weak cry. Ruari moved closer, surprised to see it was a newborn pup struggling to move in the high grasses.

Not wishing to offend the mother, he didn't pick it up right away, instead walking around the area in search for the dog or other puppies. He didn't find anything, so he picked the wee animal up and cuddled it against his chest. "My, you're nearly as cold as my mother's hand. I must warm you up. In fact, mayhap I'll go to the kitchens and get you some goat's milk. Are you the runt and your mother left you?"

The soft brown puppy mewed like a kitten as it cuddled against him, settling in his hand with a contented sigh. He shrugged his shoulder and headed toward the kitchens behind the keep. He ran into Aedan's wife, Jennie, who said, "Uh-oh, Mama left him to die, 'struth?"

"I guess so. He was struggling under the bushes." His other hand drifted to the top of the pup's head, patting him affectionately.

"Sad," Jennie said, a sadness in her gaze as she petted the animal's side. "I just saw his mother move her pups to another spot. She'll never feed him, but I'll not leave him to die. Do you want me to find one of the lassies to feed him?" Jennie glanced around the courtyard in search of either of her daughters.

Ruari was surprised to find himself shaking his head. "Nay, I'll take care of him."

"Fresh goat's milk inside." Jennie pointed to the kitchens and headed out toward the front of the curtain wall. "You need a companion, Ruari," she called over her shoulder. "You'll take good care of him."

Ruari lifted the wee dog so he could look him in the face. "Aye, I will. Now I just wish to find a name for you." He stared into the dog's eyes as his paw came up to touch his face. "You look like a Heckie to me, laddie. Heckie you are."

Once he fed the pup, he tucked him inside his tunic to warm him up, and Heckie fell asleep instantly.

Ruari knew it was foolish, but his heart warmed at the sight. He had a new friend, and somehow the world seemed a brighter place for it.

CHAPTER FOUR

JULIANA CHEWED ON THE BREAD Joan had brought her. "This is fine bread. 'Tis quite delicious."

Her sister hadn't taken a seat since returning to the room. Her stance seemed almost nervous. Mayhap she was feeling the distance between them, too. "I'll find you more if you like," Joan said.

"Nay, I'm fine. I'm nearly full. I'm sure I will be once I finish the cheese." She glanced around the small chamber, wondering if this was where her sister spent most of her day. It seemed quite dour.

Perhaps becoming a nun was not the best path for her.

"So who is it Papa wishes you to marry? Or is he just looking for a match for you?"

Juliana took a bite of her bread to keep from answering quickly because somehow she knew, no matter what the answer was, it would not suit her sister. Of course, it did not exactly suit her either, and there was no real reason to hide the truth. Joan hadn't been home for so long she probably did not know the man anyway. "Ailbeart Munro."

Joan jolted. "Munro? He's more than two decades older than you." She sat down on the bed, and Juliana could see her hands were shaking.

"He came to visit with Papa not long ago. They spoke for over an hour, and Papa seemed quite happy after he left. He didn't mention the betrothal for a while, but a few days later, he admitted he'd agreed to give my hand to Munro. He's a laird, as you know, so Papa believes 'tis a good match. The laird lost his last wife. He wishes to have sons before 'tis too late. He's had no bairns at all." She looked Joan in the eye. "I begged Papa to let me visit you so that we might discuss everything. He walked out of the room without answering me, and I felt certain he wouldn't allow it. Then, two days later, he said he'd arranged the visit."

Joan patted her hand. "He must have gotten my message. And thought your suggestion had merit." They were both quiet for a moment, then Joan said, "Please be honest, Juliana. What think you of marriage?"

Juliana played with her last pieces of food, unsure of how to answer her sister. The truth was she didn't know how she felt.

Her sire wished for her to marry a man five and twenty years older than she was.

Her sister wished for her to become a nun.

What if she wished for neither of those paths?

"I'm not sure. I'm not interested in marrying Ailbeart because he's so old. I've heard he is nice-looking, distinguished, but I'd prefer someone closer to my age. I've seen him from a distance, but I haven't met him yet, so how can I know for sure? Mayhap I'll fall in love with him."

Her sister declared with vehemence, "You will *not* fall in love with him."

"Do you know him?" She couldn't stop the sudden pitter-patter in her heart at the prospect of learning more about her possible betrothed. Why would no one tell her more about him?

"Of course I know him. He is our neighbor. How do you not know him? Did Papa tell you more about his marriage?"

"His wife died six moons ago. The only other thing Da told me was he's desperate for sons. He doesn't wish to wait because he's getting on in years."

Joan scoffed. "'Tis a ridiculous request. Papa only wishes for you to marry him because he's a laird and has money. Nay, you do not need to marry an old man just for Papa to gain coin. Tell our sire you wish to become a nun and you can stay here with me forever. He wouldn't dare tear you from the convent. 'Tis why he was reluctant to keep his promise to me."

"You think Papa would allow it? I don't think he would be pleased to tell Munro he was canceling the betrothal. And he said you trained somewhere else…would I have to leave?"

"True, you would have to train at Stonecroft Abbey. I'll take you there in another day or two so you can see what 'tis like. There are so many novices there and you'll feel right at home." She turned to Juliana and took both of her hands.

"But there's something I don't understand, Joan," she said hesitantly. How could she explain this to her sister without offending her? In her eyes, being a nun sounded quite boring.

"Then ask me. 'Tis why you came, is it not? What is it?"

She squirmed on the bed to consider her phrasing, but then blurted it out. "What does a nun do all day?"

Joan laughed, a sweet sound she rarely heard from her, though she remembered it well from childhood. Her sister had always made her laugh because she was so loving, so bubbly. This felt more like the Joan she remembered. But moments later, the laughter faded and the proper nun was back.

Joan smoothed her skirt. "It depends. Some nuns pray most of the day, others prefer to do God's work. I work with novices, which is something you could train to do. Sometimes we work with orphans, or you could become the cook of the abbey, or teach others to read. Reading the Bible is a much-needed skill. You could visit with the sick or those dying. There are so many choices. 'Tis the beauty of becoming a nun."

Juliana thought for a moment, mulling over the possibilities she'd been given. While she wouldn't mind doing some of those activities occasionally, she couldn't deny that she longed for a family of her own.

But she would never be allowed to choose her own husband. It was Ailbeart or no one.

"I'll think on it, Joan. I'm verra tired. I think I'll go to bed."

"Of course. Your journey must have been exhausting." Her sister stood and said, "I'll find you a basin of water to freshen up with before you go to bed. We'll talk more about your vocation in the morning." She kissed her cheek and left her.

Joan obviously cared about her, which was nice, but she was being as forceful as their father. If they loved her, shouldn't they care about her happiness?

Juliana suddenly felt very alone.

Ruari headed out to the lists the following day. As soon as he moved down the steps of the keep, he found a grassy patch and set his new friend down to take care of its needs.

Brin chased out behind him. "A puppy? Where did you find that one? Mama said I'm too young to have one yet."

His nephew was a good lad—hard-working with a big heart and plenty of good looks from both sides of the family, but he was smaller than the other lads his age, something that frustrated Brin to no end.

"'Tis the runt. I found him left in the bushes, his mother long gone, so I picked him up. I'm sure you'll get one as soon as they're older. Or if you work hard, I may gift this one to you in a day or two. First, we must see that he's well fed with goat's milk."

"May I pick him up? Or will he pish on me?"

Ruari barked a short laugh. "Dogs will not pish on you. They know better."

"How?" Brin gave him a curious look he knew well. The lad had been asking the question "why" ever since he'd turned three winters. He'd always loved the lad's curiosity, although he knew his nieces, who were both older, tired of it.

"I can't answer that question, Brin. Dogs sense more than most animals. I'm not sure why, but he knew enough to hold it."

The two watched the pup as he circled and sniffed, looking for just the right spot. When he finally let go, Brin giggled. "He had to go, did he not?"

"Aye, he did."

Brin picked him up and giggled as the puppy licked his cheek. "What did you name him?"

"Heckie." As Ruari watched the two become acquainted, the desire to have his own bairns washed over him. He was quick to bury it down deep. He would have to be satisfied with two beautiful nieces and one nephew. "Come, lad. Bring him along. We're off to the lists."

He turned to head out the gates, and nearly ran into his brother. "Good morn to you."

"Good timing," Aedan said, "I was looking for you both. I need a few men to escort a group to Stonecroft Abbey. There's a group of nuns who wish to travel there later today. 'Tis only about a three-hour trip. I thought I'd send you to lead, Ruari. Take Brin with you. Neil will go as well."

Ruari thought he must have heard his brother wrong. "You want me to lead with Neil along?"

"Aye. I already told Neil 'tis my preference. He said he'd gladly go."

A feather could have blown Ruari over, but he didn't have time to consider what had just happened. Brin was practically bursting with excitement.

"And I may go, too, Papa?"

"Aye, 'tis time to start sending you on guard duty. You'll listen to everything Ruari and Neil tell you or you'll not go again for a while. Understood?"

The lad's face lit up with a contagious exuberance. "I promise to be good," he said. "I will, Uncle Ruari." The lad handed him the puppy carefully, and immediately began to bounce up and down with sheer excitement. Ruari understood. He'd felt the same way when he was a lad. Any chance to travel with the guards was sheer pleasure.

Aedan set his hand on his son's shoulder and said, "Go say your goodbyes to your mama and to Grandmama. Tell them when you're going and where. 'Tis important that someone always knows when the guards and warriors take their leave."

"Aye, Papa," he said over his shoulder as he raced toward the keep.

Ruari was so stunned that he didn't know what to say to his brother.

"I don't send my only son with just anyone, Ruari," Aedan said. "Keep that in mind. You might need to leave your new friend behind." He tipped his head toward Heckie with a smile.

"I'll keep him close. His mother rejected him, so I've adopted him."

Aedan just set his hands on his hips and grinned.

"My thanks, Aedan." He didn't know what else to say, but he wished to acknowledge his appreciation for his brother's trust in him. Perhaps his brother did believe in him after all.

He'd have to prove himself on this journey.

CHAPTER FIVE

————

JULIANA FOLLOWED HER SISTER OUT of the abbey, carrying her small satchel with two extra gowns and her personals tucked inside. A handsome young lad immediately rushed over and reached for it.

"Here, my lady. I'll take care of that for you." He could only be ten or twelve summers at most, but he was most enthusiastic. He stopped suddenly and spun back around to face her. "Which horse is yours?"

Juliana smiled at him and pointed to her mare. "The chestnut one with the white markings on her face."

"Right away, my lady."

"What's your name?" she called after him.

He spun around again, so quickly she wondered if it had made him dizzy. "Brin Cameron," he said. "I'll take care of everything for you. Shall I help you mount?"

"Nay, I'll use the mount over there." She couldn't help but wonder if he *could* assist her. He wasn't overly tall for his age. Her gaze traveled over the rest of the dozen or so guards preparing to escort them, but it stopped as soon as she saw him.

Him. The handsome one who'd saved her from the reivers. His red hair was quite tousled this morn, but her attention was drawn to the way he was cooing to something in his hand.

She followed Brin over to her horse, then whispered to him, "What is that man doing?"

Brin looked at the redhead. "My uncle Ruari?" he said, much too loudly, "he's got a new puppy."

Her embarrassment faded in an instant, and she found her legs hurrying her over to Ruari's side. A fuzzy brown creature was cradled in his hand, its entire body moving as it exuberantly wagged its tail.

"A puppy? Truly?" she asked, unable to contain her own excitement.

"Aye," Ruari said, smiling at her. "His name is Heckie. Would you like to hold him, my lady?"

"Please call me Juliana, my lord. We met before, and Brin reminded me that your name is Ruari. I'm pleased you'll be escorting us to the abbey, my lord. You are the laird's brother, aye?" She gave a brief curtsy.

"No need to be so formal with me, Lady Juliana. I was about to put Heckie down to take care of his needs before we mount up, but you can pet him if you'd like." She stroked the dog's fur, savoring in his softness and the tiny yips he made.

"I like the name," she said as Ruari set him down in the grass. "Heckie is perfect for him. Is he going with you? Do you have a basket for him?"

Ruari chuckled. "Nay. He'll ride right here," he said, patting his chest. "His mother rejected him so he's quite young. I wish to keep him warm."

Juliana couldn't stop herself from staring at the man's chest, and her mouth went dry at the thought of being curled up against the heat of this man. Did he have hair on his chest? She'd seen the men practicing without shirts in the lists. Her next thought was whether it would be red or dark. Perhaps blond?

The grin he gave her made her blush. Had he guessed her thoughts? She turned around and headed back to her horse, more than surprised to find herself airborne a few seconds later. She barely had time to register that Ruari had picked her up—his hands were around her middle!—

when he tossed her onto her dear horse's saddle.

She landed with an oof, grabbing Winnie's mane.

"My apologies, I intended to be more gentle."

An older man she recognized from the other day came up behind him. "Forgive him," he said in a condescending tone that reminded her of her father. "He may look like a man, but he has the mind of a lad still." Why was he being so critical of Ruari?

She didn't miss the glare Ruari gave him. Nor did she blame him.

Brin scurried up behind the older man, staring up at him. "Uncle Ruari knows what's best, Neil. Why would you say that?"

The lad's affection for his uncle was as obvious as the older man's disdain. Her gaze shifted to Joan, who'd stayed silent through the whole exchange. Her sister was watching everything with a distant gaze.

Another horse flew into the gathering, stirring up a cloud of dust. Neil held his arm up across his eyes and bellowed, "Padraig, could you not be a little more cautious?"

Padraig gave him a crooked grin and said, "Nay. Wanted to make sure you all know I'm here. I'm going along with you." He jumped off his horse and bowed toward Juliana with a dramatic swish of his arm. "My lady, you can trust that Ruari, Brin, and I will get you to the abbey safely."

She didn't miss the way the older man glared at Padraig, nor the way he stomped off to his horse.

"Are you two related?" she asked. "But not from the same clan?" They wore different red plaids, something she'd noticed that first day.

"I'm from Clan Grant, fostering here with my cousin and Clan Cameron," Padraig said. "But I'll see that you have a most enjoyable visit." He winked at her and headed back to his horse, the others all mounting and readying their mounts.

Joan rode up to her. "You need to watch out for him,"

she said in an undertone.

"The lad named Padraig? But why? He seemed nice."

"Because he was flirting with you. Beware lads who flirt or smile at you. Or ones who try to help you." Joan's gaze traveled from Padraig to Ruari and Brin, before shifting to Neil and the rest of the guards. "You must be careful."

Juliana liked talking to the lads. Although some men were stern and unapproachable, she hadn't found that to be the case with the Camerons she'd met, and Padraig was the most high-spirited person she'd ever met. But she didn't know how to say that to Joan, at least not this stricter version of Joan, and so she simply responded with a slight nod. Her gaze shot to Ruari, who'd mounted and taken his position at the head of the group. He spoke to the guards, assigning them various positions, then turned to them. "Ladies, 'tis a three-hour journey. If all is well, we'll stop after two hours for a wee break. This should ensure our arrival will be before dark." He then tucked the puppy inside his tunic and motioned for the group to move.

If she could travel next to Ruari, she'd be as pleased as that pup, although that was a thought she could decidedly not share with her sister.

As Ruari led the group out, he positioned himself exactly where he wished to be.

Close to Juliana.

Heckie fell asleep against his chest, so he didn't need to worry about him, but he kept panning the area for possible marauders or reivers. He didn't expect any trouble along the way, but that could change at a moment's notice.

An hour into their journey, Juliana found her way up near his horse. "My lord Cameron?"

"Ruari, you mean?" He cast a sideways glance toward her, doing his best to maintain his view of the glen ahead of them.

"As you wish, Ruari, but you are leading this charge so you should demand respect."

"I prefer to earn respect," he said, "but I appreciate your thoughtfulness. Did you have a question?"

"I'm just worried about the puppy. Do you not think we should stop for him?" He noticed her staring at his upper arms, something he hadn't expected from such an innocent lass. One who was considering becoming a novice, no less.

He also caught her glancing at her sister to see if she was watching her.

She was indeed.

"I'll not stop for just a pup," Ruari said. "Are you trying to tell me you may need to stop?" He didn't look at her as he said it, because he was quite sure she'd blush at his comment.

Brin, who was riding right behind him, let out a bark of laughter, something lads often did when discussing private habits with lasses. Ruari glared at his nephew over his shoulder, something that quickly silenced him.

"Nay, I'm fine," she said with a hasty retort…and a shade of red he hadn't seen in a while traveled up her neck and across her cheeks.

In fact, he'd embarrassed her enough that she dropped her horse back behind him, which he hadn't wanted to happen. But mayhap it was for the best. Neil was keeping his gaze on everything Ruari did, eager to find fault.

Half an hour later, Ruari came upon an area with some good cover, a place where the ladies could relieve themselves without damaging their tender sensibilities. Lifting his hand, he slowed his horse and glanced back at Padraig and Neil. "Quarter-hour break."

Within minutes, Juliana and her sister were headed off into the bushes. Brin ran into the bushes ahead of the rest of them, and all Ruari could do was shake his head. He could remember being Brin's age, when everything in the world looked bright. He'd lost that feeling a long time ago.

Perhaps it had happened shortly into his marriage.

He took care of his own needs, then awakened Heckie and set him down in the grass to do his business.

Most of the others were busy off in the bushes, but Juliana approached him, her eyes on Heckie. She lifted him and cuddled him close to her bosom, giving him the unsettling feeling of being jealous of a dog, but he didn't let his gaze linger. His focus was on their surroundings.

Their group had scattered. A bad feeling came upon him, but before he had time to shout out a warning, four horses charged at them, sending Juliana in a panic because one of them was headed straight for her.

Ruari didn't think. He acted. He bellowed for his men to mount up, tossed her up onto his horse, and climbed on behind her, sending the stallion in the opposite direction of the attacking reivers.

Yelling back over his shoulder, he said, "Brin! Hide behind Padraig."

He rounded a section of the glen and was fortunate to find a group of trees behind a rock formation large enough to conceal them, even with his horse.

His brain was in a turmoil. He was the leader of the group. Should he have left Juliana and gone after the reivers, or had he done the right thing getting her away from them?

He honestly didn't know, but he'd made his choice.

She turned around and buried her face in his chest with a whimper, and he wrapped his arm around her, just then looking down to see the pup still in her grip. "Heckie, you better say thank you to the lass for saving you. Those horses would have trampled you in no time." He hoped talking about the animal would distract her from any shedding any tears.

She leaned back to look at Ruari. "I fear I'll squish him."

Heckie gave a high-pitched yip and she laughed, a sound that was as sweet as anything he'd ever heard.

"I think you saved him."

"Who are those men?" she asked, looking up at him with such awe and trust it humbled him. Her face paled as the sounds of battle carried to them over the rocks, her gaze shifting toward the cacophony.

He had to distract her. He couldn't have her fainting and falling off his horse. "Juliana, look at me." His finger reached for her chin to turn her face back toward him. Reluctantly, she complied.

"Who are they?" Her eyes drifted back toward the battle as yelps of pain filled the air.

"Reivers of some kind would be my guess." He cupped her cheek and turned her back toward him again.

Meeting his gaze, she whispered, "I don't like this. Why are more men attacking us? I thought the abbeys were supposed to be safe."

He could see the misting of tears in her eyes. "'Tis most difficult to watch and hear such violence, especially if you are not accustomed to it," he said softly, wishing he could shield her from it. "We were afraid there would be more reivers about now that the Channel of Dubh has been ended."

"The Channel of Dubh?"

He couldn't believe she'd never heard of it, but it was clear her father had kept her hidden from the world. "There was a large group of men who were involved with selling young lads and lasses across the water."

"Selling them for what?"

He wouldn't poison her innocence by telling her. "'Tis not important. The group paid unsavory characters to work for them, but a group of young Highlanders put an end to them."

"'Tis good news, is it not?" she asked, cuddling Heckie under her chin.

"Aye, but that means there are more men looking for coin."

She leaned toward Ruari and whispered, "But they wouldn't kidnap me, would they? What would they want with me?"

Ruari nearly groaned at her thoughts, wondering at the same time why no one had told her about men and women and the ways of the world. Instead of thinking about how he could answer her, he stared at her pink lips, plump and ready for him and a scant breath away from his own. He could just have a quick taste…

"Juliana!"

Joan's voice carried across the glen. He'd been so entranced with Juliana's lips that he hadn't noticed that the sounds of battle had dissipated.

Starting, he turned her around and grabbed the reins, guiding his horse back in the direction of the battle. Neil, Padraig, Brin, and Joan were all on horseback. Padraig was bloodied up quite a bit, but Neil and Joan appeared fine. Brin looked ecstatic.

"Brin, you are hale?" He had to bring his nephew back to safety or his brother would kill him.

Brin nodded. "'Twas so exciting! I stayed with Padraig just as you said, Uncle Ruari."

"All survived?" he asked, his gaze surveying the rest of the guards. Everyone appeared to be present, although some of the men were still joining them.

"Aye, our men survived, not the others," Neil said. "We took care of the reivers, but where the hell were you? You're in charge of the group."

Ruari didn't like being accused of negligence in front of everyone, so he just said, "Aye, I am in charge. My decision was to protect an innocent lass from a group of reivers and I accomplished my goal. You all have fared well, so clearly I did not make a mistake."

His tone was brusque enough that no one said anything except Joan. "And what did you do to my sister back there?"

THE BANISHED HIGHLANDER   45

Her tone was even more accusatory than Neil's had been. "What did I *do*? Naught. I protected her. 'Tis my job."

"Joan! What are you saying?" Juliana asked. "He protected me. We did naught else. We hid in the trees until the fighting was over. And I was pleased with his protection. Those men…one came straight toward me."

"Where is your horse?" Joan asked.

Juliana's eyes widened as she glanced about. Her lower lip started to tremble. "Nay, did they hurt my horse? Winnie?"

"Nay, they wouldn't have," Ruari said. "She's probably hiding or perhaps she's run off."

Padraig said, "I didn't notice your horse, but sometimes they'll return to where they started."

Ruari instructed four of their men to search for the beast, and they quickly fanned out to do so. Several moments later, they returned, shaking their heads.

"No horse anywhere, my lord."

"Then Juliana will ride with me until we arrive at the abbey," Ruari said. "We'll search for your horse on the way back to Cameron land. There could be more reivers out there, so I don't wish to spend any more time here. We move on."

Although he wished the mare would be found for Lady Juliana's sake, he didn't mind the prospect of riding behind her for the rest of the journey—if he could stand to have her sweet backside moving against him for so long.

Neil said, "Finally, you made a good decision. We all move forward. Those men were after something, but I don't know what."

Ruari glanced at Neil, but he said nothing.

He didn't want Juliana or Joan to guess what the reivers had been after.

It was either one of the lasses or both of them.

CHAPTER SIX

ONCE THEY ARRIVED AT STONECROFT Abbey, Juliana thanked Ruari for protecting her, but she barely had time to get the words out before her sister dragged her away. Joan yanked on her arm so hard, she could barely keep up with her.

"Joan, please slow down," she whispered in an undertone. "You're hurting me."

Joan ignored her pleas and continued to yank her along until they were inside the abbey, the door slamming shut behind them. A nun in the foyer took one look at Joan's face and turned away, rushing down the passageway.

"Joan, what's wrong?" She had no idea what had possessed her sister to act so strangely.

"What's wrong?" Joan barked. "You were alone with that man on top of a horse, then you rode in front of him the whole way here. You were too close!" The expression on her face was one of sheer fury. She'd never seen her sister like this before.

A feeling of misgiving stole over her. Joan had changed even more than she'd thought.

"My horse disappeared. Believe me, I would rather have had my dear mare to ride, but she's gone and I don't know if I'll ever see her again." Her voice hitched as she said it.

Joan let out a deep sigh and closed her eyes, her lips moving as if she were counting.

Or was she praying?

"Joan?"

"Juliana, you don't understand the way of men. You were at great risk of being molested by that man. You should never have allowed him to take you away from the group."

"But one of the reivers was coming straight at me. I fear what could have happened had he grabbed me. Ruari saved me. He did naught wrong."

Joan's hands grabbed her by the shoulders, a punishingly tight grip that frightened her. "Ruari? Did he try to kiss you?"

Juliana thought of how close their lips had been at one time. The truth was she'd wished for him to kiss her, but they'd been interrupted. She stared off at the columns in the passageway, wondering exactly how his lips would have tasted. Although she'd never been kissed before, she guessed it would have been quite delicious…

"Juliana!"

She whipped her face back to her sister, blushing at her thoughts.

"He *did* kiss you! I can see it in your face. You must go and beg the Lord's forgiveness. You must pray for the rest of the eve."

"Joan, nay. He did not kiss me. Please stop this." She gasped as her gaze caught a wet patch on the fabric over her sister's thigh. "Joan," she pointed. "You're bleeding. You were cut. Oh, dear, you must sit down. Mistress Jennie is back on Cameron land. Is she the one they spoke of? Is she a healer…" She spun in a circle, desperate to find help, as her sister glanced down at her wound. "But she's not here."

"Oh…oh…" Joan grasped for Juliana's hand, her knees buckling.

"Help! Please, someone help." The door flew open and the man named Neil came in and caught Joan just before she collapsed to the ground in a dead faint.

"Sister!" Neil shouted. "We need assistance."

Three nuns rushed down the passageway, one ahead of the other two. "In here, bring her in here. There's a pallet for her."

Juliana followed helplessly as Neil carried Joan into a small chamber and carefully settled her onto the pallet, taking a moment to study her wound through the gown. "Get a healer. She needs to get that tended or she'll have the fever."

A strong presence filled the room, and without even looking, she knew Ruari had joined them. She took a step back and leaned against his chest, grateful to have his support, needful of his touch. His hand settled on her hip, to her surprise, but she had no desire for him to move it.

Her world had crumbled apart in just a matter of a few hours.

Attacked twice by reivers, her horse lost to her, Joan chastising her, and now her dear sister had fainted from her wound.

Neil yelled out, "I said find a healer!"

What would befall her next?

Fix this. You must fix this for her.

The answer came to him in a trice. His niece Tara was visiting the abbey, teaching some of the novices the basic art of healing. "My niece is here," he announced. "I'll go for her. She's probably in the back where the novices are." He hurried out and darted down the passageway to the area for residents in the back.

As he headed down the long passageway, he bellowed, "Tara Cameron. Your healing skills are needed."

Tara popped out at the end of the passageway. "Uncle Ruari?" she called out in surprise. "What brings you here? You're not here to take me home, are you?"

"Nay, but your healing skills are needed. You need to sew a wound closed and put your mother's poultice on it so it won't fester." He motioned for her to go after her supplies. "Please do not tarry. One of the sisters was injured in a battle with reivers."

Three more young lasses hurried into the passageway as Tara disappeared from view to grab her satchel.

"Which sister?" asked one, her face clearly worried.

"Sister Joan. We brought her sister Juliana with her, but we were attacked along the way."

One novice broke into tears, while another said, "We'll help tend to her." The other two lasses nodded vehemently, although the first had not yet stopped crying.

"Nay, there are enough people there," Ruari objected. "You may see her later after she rests. Her sister and Tara will take good care of her." He could just imagine what chaos would erupt if the three lasses followed him. They appeared to be between the ages of ten and twelve summers.

Tara returned to the passageway with her satchel. "I'll see to her and come back to update you. I'm sure she'll be fine."

Ruari couldn't help but smile at his niece's delicate way of handling the situation. At six and ten, she was nearly a woman grown. She reminded him of her mother. Like Jennie, she had a wonderful ability to soothe the people around her. She even looked like her mother with the same color hair and the same deep brown eyes, although she had a few more freckles across her nose due to her love for horseback riding.

"Come along, King," he said. His niece was part Irish, on Aedan's side, and Jennie had looked to Irish lore when choosing her name. Many of the High Kings had also carried the title King of Tara, in reference to the famed Hill of Tara in Ireland, which was the genesis for Tara's nickname. Ruari had gotten in the habit of calling her "King" when she was young, as she'd always been the leader among her group of lasses.

"Uncle Ruari, please stop," she said, blushing a faint pink as she hustled ahead of him, hurrying down the passageway at a rapid pace. "I have much to do."

"She's not seriously hurt, but she does need your poultice."

Tara flashed her brilliant smile at him, and it struck him, not for the first time, that his niece was all grown up. Soon she would want to marry, and he would have to help Aedan ensure the men who courted her were suitable.

Brin came flying down the passageway, shouting for his sister. "She needs you!"

"She's coming, Brin. Calm down," Ruari said, motioning for him to calm down. "We are in an abbey."

Brin stopped in front of his uncle, staring up at him, his face falling in a matter of seconds. "Sorry, Uncle Ruari. I was trying to be helpful."

Mayhap he'd sounded too harsh. "'Tis naught to worry about, lad. I know your intentions were good, but we must respect our surroundings. I'm sure your sister will be able to help Sister Joan."

Brin nodded, but Ruari noticed the way his shoulders drooped as he walked—slowly—back toward the front of the abbey, Tara slipping in front of him.

Guilt pressed down on Ruari. Hadn't he been just like Brin back in the day? He'd wanted so badly to help Aedan, but he'd always felt like he was in the way. Always except for that one time when his spying had proved helpful.

He didn't want to crush Brin's spirit, so he clasped his shoulder and said, "Brin, you did a fine job when we were under attack. I saw you move to the side to allow the larger warriors to do their job. The most important thing you could do was get out of the way and not make yourself a target."

"But Uncle Ruari, I was watching so I could help if anyone tried to be sneaky. One of the reivers tried to attack Padraig from behind. I warned him, and he turned around just in time and cut the bast...man down."

Pride coursed through him. So much so, he decided to ignore his nephew's near cursing. "Here, Brin," he said, reaching inside his tunic. "Why don't you take Heckie outside to romp in the grass for a wee bit."

Brin's face lit up as he cupped his hands for the puppy, carefully handling the treasure placed there.

Padraig's boots echoed on the stones as he came charging down the passageway toward them, doing exactly what Ruari had told Brin not to do "Ruari, did your nephew tell you how he saved my arse?"

Ruari gave his cousin a sharp look he hoped he understood. "Do not forget where you are."

"Och, the sisters will forgive my slip. Nonetheless," he said, reaching down to clasp Brin's shoulder. He bent down to whisper in the lad's ear. "You saved my arse and I thank you for it."

Brin's chuckles echoed up and down stone arches of the passageway, but most importantly, his shoulders had righted themselves to where they should be. One comment had changed his entire outlook on the world.

How Ruari wished the same could happen to him.

CHAPTER SEVEN

JULIANA SAT BY HER SISTER'S bed the next morning, sewing two more purple flowers into her needlework as she waited for Joan to open her eyes. She prayed her sister wouldn't suffer from fever. She'd been a little warm overnight, but her color was good this morning.

A light knock on the door caught her attention. "Come in," she said, having no idea who it was. She wished it were Ruari Cameron, but he'd gone back to Cameron land last eve.

Her excitement for the trip had diminished quite a bit after the handsome man had left. She could only hope he'd found her horse on the way home.

A young dark-haired lass cautiously opened the door, revealing two other lasses behind her. "Greetings," the leader said. "How is Sister Joan? We'd like to visit with her if we may."

Juliana set her needlework on the side table and offered her stool to the lass, but the young woman declined.

"Come in," she said, hoping their visit would awaken Joan. "She hasn't stirred this morn, but I'd be pleased to visit with you. She wished to show me the work she does here. Do you see her often?"

The dark-haired lass nodded gravely. "Aye, we see her every day when she's here at Stonecroft. Sister Joan teaches us about the Bible. My name is Anora, and this is Lavena, and Prudencia." She pointed to a tall brown-haired girl first and then a much shorter blonde.

The last girl grinned, gave a slight bow, and said, "Please call me Prudie. We've been worried about Sister Joan. Did she sleep well?"

Her sister's voice came from behind her. "I slept just fine. My dear sister, Juliana, whom I brought to visit with you, took verra good care of me." She reached for Juliana's hand and pulled her back to the stool next to the bed. Juliana stared at Joan as she sat, needing the reassurance that she was indeed hale.

"These are my lassies," Joan said. "They all study verra hard to become good interpreters of our Lord's word."

Prudie giggled, covering her mouth with her hand. She appeared to be the youngest. "And she teaches us how to cook and make pastries, my favorite. We brought one for you, Sister Joan."

Lavena produced a basket from behind her back. "Aye, fresh bread and a pastry for you." Her face beamed with pride at the offering.

"Set it down for now," Joan said with a smile. "Tell me you've been studying all along while I've been away."

Anora nodded. "We've gone through two more psalms."

"Good, Anora," Joan said. "Are you teaching them how to read their letters?"

"Aye, Sister. They are doing verra well."

"You can read?" Juliana asked in shock, glancing from the lasses to her sister. She'd always wished to read, but her papa had said women didn't need to learn. How had she not known this about her sister?

"Aye," Joan said. "When I began my studies, I would travel to Cameron land twice a sennight and Mistress Jennie would teach me. Now I teach the novices and any nun who is interested. 'Tis the best way to understand our Lord's words."

"Will you teach me how to read?" Juliana asked.

All three girls giggled at her question. "You didn't teach your own sister how to read?" Lavena said, although there was no cruelty in it—just the brutal honesty of the young.

Joan stared at Juliana, her gaze sad, then said, "Why don't you lasses return to the kitchens and help the nuns prepare the evening meal? I'd like to spend time with my sister, if you don't mind."

The three said their goodbyes and left, chattering all the way down the passageway. Joan explained, "We don't eat much at high sun. The nuns make a fine stew and breads for the evening meal. It takes many hands to chop the vegetables."

But Juliana's mind was still fixed on what the lasses had said about their reading lessons. "Why didn't you ever tell me you could read? You know I've always wished to learn."

Her sister sighed and reached for her hand. "I didn't learn until I left home, and we haven't spent enough time together since for me to teach you. This would be a good time for you to learn. I'd be happy to teach you along with the novices. Perhaps give you some private lessons. There are many things you can do if you become a nun. Learning to read is one of them."

"Must I become a nun to learn how to read?" She hoped not. Wouldn't it be a wonderful skill to have for everyone? Even lasses? She hated her sire's view of females.

Joan pushed herself up in bed and motioned for her sister to place the basket of treats close enough for her to eat something. She broke off a piece of bread and took one of the linen squares from the basket and set it on her lap. "Juliana, we must talk."

"About what? Please don't ask me about the men again. Naught happened, and you were so upset. I promise you I've never been kissed, though…"

"That pleases me. I'm sorry I was so upset. I think I was still shaken from the attack. I didn't even notice my own wound. But please finish your sentence." She took a bite of her bread and waited for Juliana to answer.

What she had to say next embarrassed her, but she didn't wish to avoid it. She needed to be honest with her sister.

"Though I might like to be kissed by someone. Joan, don't you ever wish you were married to a wonderful man? Have your own bairns?"

"Nay, I don't. I have no desire to ever have a bairn. If you knew what it involved, you wouldn't either. Someday soon, when I'm not exhausted, I must tell you about womanhood. You've had your courses, have you not?"

"Aye, but what does that have to do with having bairns?"

Her sister gave a deep groan and said, "My head hurts. We'll talk later." She lifted up the bedcover and stared at her leg. "Why don't you find someone to change the bandage?"

Juliana sighed and did as her sister asked.

Would she ever find out more about men and bairns?

———◆———

Ruari strode into Aedan's solar, Brin, Padraig, and Neil behind him. "Good eve to you, brother."

"Come in and sit down," his brother said, nodding toward the stools arranged in front of his desk, one in front of the rest. "There are enough stools. I wish to hear all that transpired. Brin's tongue has not stopped wagging since you returned. Though I thank you for bringing him back unhurt." Ruari took the stool in the front, as he'd led the mission, but Neil picked up a different stool and moved it closer to Aedan.

As if to send him a message.

Well, Ruari would ignore it. He would not allow Neil to play with his head anymore.

"The journey was uneventful until we stopped for a break an hour shy of Stonecroft Abbey. We had been there nearly a quarter of an hour when a band of four reivers broke through the trees, one headed directly toward

Juliana. I tossed her onto my horse and found a spot where I felt she was safe from danger."

Neil made a rude noise. "And you should have deposited her there and returned to fight. Your job was to protect Brin and you left him."

"I trusted you and Padraig to protect Brin, if need be, but I also had faith that he could protect himself. They were not after lads."

"And how the hell would you know what they were after? The Channel paid good coin for lads. For all we know they hoped to take up where they left off," Neil said, turning his attention away from Ruari and back to Aedan. "'Tis my opinion, Chief, that Sister Joan was wounded because Ruari ran and hid."

Aedan stared at Neil and said something uncharacteristic for him. "Neil, I'll warn you only once that you speak of my brother."

All of them fell silent at that, and Neil looked shocked at the rebuke. No more so than Ruari felt.

Padraig said, "With all respect, I have to disagree with your second, Chief. My instinct was to do just as Ruari did. When I saw the lead horse headed straight for Juliana, my belly dropped because I didn't think I could get to her in time. Ruari did exactly what I would have done. If you recall, she was grabbed by the fools on your own land. She would have been my priority, also. We handled the rest of the marauders with no problem, and Brin moved out of the way. I was grateful he took the view that he did because he warned me when one was coming from behind me. I'd have been injured for certes if not for your son."

Hellfire, the best thing Ruari had seen in days was his nephew's proud face and broad grin. If it were possible for his wee chest to puff out anymore, he would have lifted into the air. He glanced back at his brother, pleased to see his expression of pride. His brother had hoped for a son but had been blessed with two lasses first. He'd loved all of his children equally, but he did burst with satisfaction and pride whenever his son did something worthy of his attention.

Aedan was a good father. How Ruari wished he'd had the same opportunity. It was one of his keenest regrets.

Neil burst out, "Chief, the nun was struck. It shouldn't have happened."

Ruari did not rush to his own defense, instead waiting for his brother's response.

Using the low tone he reserved for his final judgments, Aedan said, "Juliana Clavelle was in our charge and has been since her guards were killed. Protecting her should have been everyone's first concern. Brin also came through uninjured. So Ruari's decision was correct. I'll ask you where Sister Joan was when she was injured, Neil?"

Neil's gaze narrowed as he stared at his laird, something that Ruari had never seen before. "She was headed toward me. I called her over so I could protect her. I did not want a lady off alone."

"Yet you judge my brother for doing the same with the younger sister?" Aedan shifted his attention to the rest of the group. "Where was Sister Joan's wound and did she survive?"

Ruari spoke up. "She had a slice across her left thigh. Tara treated her with your wife's best poultice and stitched her. I expect she is fine."

"Then this will be considered a successful journey. I'll hear no more talk of failures."

The others filed out of the solar, but Ruari hung back, waiting until Padraig closed the door. "My apologies, Aedan, if I did wrong."

"Nay, you did not," his brother said, moving closer to him. Ruari had been the taller of the two of them ever since he turned twelve summers, and he was more broad-shouldered besides. While he favored practicing in the lists, his brother had always loved looking at the stars. Or his wife. "Ignore Neil. He's getting older and he's not pleased about it. You did the right thing, and you gave my son plenty to speak about. My thanks to you. Go find yourself an ale."

"My thanks, Aedan," he said on his way out, stepping outside the door and nearly running into his other niece Riley.

Riley looked more like Aedan, and her quiet temperament also favored her sire.

"Uncle Ruari, here's your pet. I just fed him."

"My thanks, Riley." He took Heckie and tucked him inside his plaid. "Are you missing your sister?"

"Of course, but I didn't come here to ask about her. I wished to speak to you. You're not wrong," she said before she stepped into the solar to greet her sire.

He shifted slightly to look at her. "I'm not wrong about what?"

She gave him a wry smile and shrugged her shoulders, closing the door to put an end to their conversation.

CHAPTER EIGHT

RUARI HEADED OUT THE DOOR, but Riley's comment stayed with him. She'd always had an eerie sense of what was on someone's mind, but she was rarely so direct about it.

So what had he been thinking about?

Neil. It must have something to do with his brother's second. He didn't understand the extent of the man's bad animosity toward him. Maybe it was time to confront him directly.

To his surprise, Neil wasn't that far down the passageway. Had he lingered outside the door to listen?

"Neil," he called out. The man stopped his forward progress, swiveling around to face him.

"What is it? Do you intend to gloat? You needn't bother. I know Aedan will always support his only sibling."

Ruari didn't know exactly how to respond to that. It wasn't true, but he didn't wish to say so out loud, especially not to this man. Heckie nuzzled against him as if sensing he needed comfort.

"Even though he was completely wrong."

Now *that* he could respond to. "Wrong? How the hell was I wrong to protect a lass under twenty summers?"

"You lose focus. You have eyes only for her, and you lose focus on what's most important." Neil turned around and headed back down the passageway, ignoring him.

"Have eyes for whom?" The bastard could try to dismiss

him, but he wasn't going to allow it. He grabbed Neil's arm, forcing him to turn back around.

"Lady Juliana. Anyone could see you are interested in her. I just hope she doesn't end up dead like your wife."

"You've made sly comments about that before. 'Tis time for you to stop. I had naught to do with Doirin's death."

"Didn't you?" he asked.

"Explain yourself," Ruari said, clenching his jaw so hard it hurt.

Neil's voice dropped so low that only Ruari would be able to hear it. "If you hadn't argued about having bairns, she wouldn't have bolted on her horse at such a speed. You know it, and that's why you feel guilty." His gaze narrowed with condemnation. "As you should. 'Tis as if you killed her with your own sword."

That crossed the line. Ruari set Heckie down, careful not to hurt him, then leaped at Neil and grabbed him by the throat. "How the hell would you know all the details about our conversation?"

"Because I heard you arguing. I followed her because I was worried about her. You surely weren't."

"I followed her, or don't you recall? I was right behind you. My question is, why were you listening to us?"

"It was accidental. I didn't eavesdrop. I just happened to be walking by when I overheard you."

"You wait until now to tell me this?" Ruari wished to shut his mouth for good, but he knew Aedan wouldn't be happy about it if he did.

"Don't worry. I haven't told anyone. But I know the truth. There was no love between you, was there?"

"What the hell do you know about love?"

"More than you."

"You've never married."

"But I *have* loved."

Riley's words popped back into his head. *You're not wrong.* He'd often suspected that Neil had cared for his wife a wee bit too much. "Is that so? And who were those feelings for? My wife?"

Neil's blank stare neither confirmed nor denied anything.

"Or is it Lady Juliana you're after? Is that why you were so upset? Because you're interested in her?" He tossed Neil aside and brushed his hands together as if to cleanse them of dirt. "Do you not think your age difference is too much, Neil?" It surprised him how the question came out—almost as a growl. He hadn't realized Neil could rile him that much. "You're an old man. Lady Juliana would never be interested in an old man."

He had to walk away before he said something he'd regret. Leaning down to pick up Heckie, he tucked him close and glared at Neil over his shoulder before he left.

Neil's face turned serious. "You've got it all wrong, Ruari. I am not interested in Lady Juliana. She *is* too young for me."

Neil spun on the heel of his boot and stalked away without another word.

He hadn't denied being interested in Doirin, had he?

———◆———

Later that eve, Juliana sat in her sister's chamber. She'd listened to Joan's chastisements for the better part of the day. While she'd pushed her sister to explain why she didn't wish to have bairns, she'd always skirted the issue, saying she'd explain once they left the abbey.

Finally, she got the courage up to ask her dear sister the question that had always lurked in the crevices of her mind. "That day when I was eight winters and you argued with Papa... Who was it he wished for you to marry, and why did you choose to become a nun instead?" She folded her hands in her lap, her gaze on her sister, expectantly waiting for an answer.

The color drained out of Joan's face, and she reached for the coverlet on the bed and pulled it up to her chin.

"Go now. Leave me. Please find me an ale. I don't wish…I cannot…" Her hand waved at her and Juliana saw the misting in her eyes.

Why would such a simple question make her cry?

Not wanting to upset her sister anymore, she bolted off her stool and moved to the door, pausing to say, "Forgive me, Joan. Is there anything else I can get for you?"

Her sister averted her gaze and shook her head.

Juliana closed the door as quietly as possible, then found her way down the stone passageway, glancing up at the ornate etchings on the columns she passed. Occasionally, a spider's web waved at her from a dark corner, but she had no interest in killing the wee beasties.

Let them live. They'd do nothing to hurt her.

The sound of her slippers hitting the stone floor echoed down the length of the passageway. At the end, she took the steps down to the great hall, shivering as she entered the lofty common chamber. The stone abbey was uncommonly cold, the hearths few and far between.

The young lasses who'd visited Joan had been heading toward the main door, but they turned to greet her as she walked in.

"How is Sister Joan?" Prudie asked. "Is she much improved? I do miss her."

"She's much better." She forced a smile for her sister's students.

"May we visit with her?"

"I'm sure she'd be pleased to see you. Go right ahead and tell her I'll be there in a few moments."

Prudie and Lavena left, but Anora, the dark-haired one, held back. "Go on," she said to her friends. "I'll catch up with you."

The two hurried toward the staircase at the end of the hall. Juliana pointed to the empty grouping of chairs in front of the blazing hearth. "Do you mind? 'Tis a wee bit drafty for me."

Anora nodded and followed her to the end of the hall. Juliana stood in front of the roaring fire, holding her hands in front of her to toast them. She detested the cold, and always had. Her chamber at home had seemed so much colder after Joan had left, mayhap because they'd always shared their bed.

What an odd revelation.

She settled in the chair and smiled at Anora, hoping the lass would tell her why she'd stayed back. She didn't have to wait long.

Anora's smile was so bright, it radiated light like a sunbeam. "I hope you do not mind, but I wished to ask you a question. If 'tis too forward, please let me know and I'll take my leave."

"Please ask me anything you'd like. I'll answer if I can," she said, silently basking in the heat of the fire like a kitten being tended by its mother.

"I wondered if you could tell me why you wish to become a nun," the lass said, leaning forward, obviously anxious to hear her answer.

Juliana hadn't expected that question. She'd not been around many young lads and lasses, but she found their youth invigorating. Their innocent joy touched her, and their honesty made her wish to be better. But why had Anora asked her such a question? "I haven't decided for certes, but my sister loves her vocation so she has tried to convince me to take my vows. What about you?"

"Prudie and I have always lived here. It's assumed we'll take our vows. She's sure 'tis what she wants, but I'm curious." She kneaded her hands in her lap, clearly uncomfortable with the subject of their conversation.

"What are you curious about?"

Anora blushed and whispered, "About lads. Are you not curious?" The poor lass glanced over her shoulder as if she feared being overheard. She probably didn't have anyone to ask about lads if her sister was as averse to the topic with them as she was with her.

Could she be honest with a stranger? Why not? Her sister refused to hear her out, but Anora had sought an audience with her. She took a deep breath and spoke her mind. "Aye, 'struth is I am verra interested in lads, but Joan doesn't wish for me to discuss it."

"Lavena and I tried to ask her about kissing one day, but she wasn't interested in talking about it. She must not have any experience with boys. What say you?" Anora's eyes were brown, the color of chestnuts.

"I haven't much experience either, but I'm attracted to the prospect of loving someone and having bairns of my own. I'm just not sure if being a nun is right for me." She could see the excitement building in Anora at the mere mention of lads. Surely such a lass didn't belong in an abbey. "How did you come to live in an abbey? Your parents sent you at such a young age?"

Anora shook her head, then chewed on her fingernail before she spoke. "Prudie and I are orphans. We were found in baskets and brought here."

"Together?"

"Nay, about six moons apart. Prudie likes to say we're true sisters." She chewed on her fingernail again, then covered her hands as if embarrassed by her habit.

"Mayhap you are. 'Tis a lovely idea. Would that not please you?"

Anora looked over at a group of nuns still eating at one of the trestle tables. "Aye. 'Tis hard not knowing where you came from. My mother died birthing me and my sire didn't wish to raise me alone, so he brought me here. The nuns accepted me."

"I'm sorry to hear that. Do you wish to leave the abbey?"

"I think I would like to travel somewhere new. I've never been anywhere but the abbey."

"Will they not allow you?"

"The abbess told me that I can leave when I turn six

and ten. They have a list of places I can go. Mayhap to Edinburgh. The abbeys are larger when you go farther south, and there are many people who work in them who are not nuns or priests. They cook or clean. Mayhap I'd like to try that. I…I don't know."

"Does my sister know of your wish?" Joan wouldn't tolerate any talk of Juliana leaving, but surely she would understand this young lass's wish to see something more of the world.

"Aye, but she says 'tis up to the abbess," she replied, chewing on her fingernail again. She looked unhappy, Juliana realized, as if she were counting the days until she would turn six and ten.

"Anora," she said, reaching for her hand. "Promise me that you'll go. You deserve to see more of the world before you decide what to do with your life. No one should be able to make that decision except for you."

Anora's face brightened. "Thank you for saying so. How about you? What will you decide?"

The first thing that surfaced in Juliana's mind was a broad-shouldered man with dark red hair.

But how was she to see him again?

CHAPTER NINE

R UARI HEADED TO THE LISTS with Padraig, determined to practice his sword skills until his hands bled. Mayhap he could best Neil by proving he was better than him. Brin tagged along, something he often did of late. Though the laddie wasn't quite capable of swinging a full-sized sword yet, he worked hard, as hard as any of the men in the Cameron lists.

Unfortunately, Ruari's mind kept drifting to a sweet lass with light brown hair that shone like honey in the light of the mid-day sun.

Padraig noticed and teased him. "I'm thinking your vision is clouded by a nice curvaceous pair of hips."

Ruari growled and swung harder at his sparring partner.

"Och, I hit the mark." He chuckled. "Or have I just grown a nice pair of breasts that are calling to you?"

Ruari burst into laughter, stepping back to keep himself from getting struck.

Padraig lowered his sword arm and puffed his chest out. "I have, haven't I?" He changed his position, bending at the waist and puckering his lips. "Or are you of a mind to kiss my sweet lips?" He closed his eyes and made smacking sounds with his mouth.

Ruari got his laughter under control and leaned against a tree next to them, crossing his arms. "Let me know when you're ready to be a true threat, lass, because you've a ways to go."

Padraig strolled about in a slow circle, attempting to sway his hips like a lass. The spectacle made Ruari laugh again, and it also caught the attention of Brin, who'd been busy playing with Heckie.

"What are you doing, Padraig?" the lad asked, looking up at him with wide eyes. "Why are you walking so oddly? Did you hurt yourself?"

"Nay, he's afraid to spar with me, Brin," Ruari said with a grin. "Ignore him."

Brin shrugged and shifted his attention back to Heckie.

Padraig grinned, and Ruari moved away from the tree and said, "I'll focus if you'll stop your taunting."

It was indeed difficult, but he had come up with the perfect way to focus. Every time Juliana surfaced in his thoughts, he forced himself to think of Padraig swaying his hips.

For the next two days, Ruari devoted himself to practice, but on the third morning, he knew it was time to visit his mother. It had been too long. Taking in a deep, heartening breath, he made his way to the tower room where she spent most of her time. It pained him to see that she was still abed. "Mama, are you hale?"

"Ruari, of course I am. Come in and chat with me for a wee bit. I haven't seen Brin, but that sweet Tara stopped by to visit with me."

He kissed his mother's cheek and pulled up a stool. "Mama, why do you have a bandage on your arm?"

"I bumped into something last eve. Jennie took care of it for me. What would I do without her?"

"Are you sure Tara didn't put the bandage there? Mayhap 'tis why she visited with you."

"Do not be ridiculous. Jennie is the healer, not Tara. Tara, Riley, and Brin come to see me every day. They're my blood."

"Either way, you've been fixed up. Please be careful when

you move about. Did you not have the tallow lit?"

"I did. Or I was trying to light it. Perhaps that's what happened."

She stared off into space.

"Mama, you look tired. I'm going out to the lists. Do you need anything?"

"Nay," she replied, blindly staring at the wall as if lost in some dream of her own making.

He stood up to leave, but her hand grasped his arm. "Ruari, 'tis not your fault. Aedan was born first, so he was destined to be chieftain. He's stronger."

He chuckled at the oft-repeated platitude. "I know, Mama. You need not worry about me. I accepted it a long time ago."

"Did you?"

"Aye, stop thinking on it." He blew her a kiss and hurried out the door, not wanting to take the discussion any further than that. On his way out, he stopped by the hearth in the great hall to check on Heckie, who was cuddled up in the small crate he'd left out for him. When he picked the puppy up, Heckie nuzzled against his chest. "Do you sleep all day, wee one?"

Heckie yawned and settled inside the plaid strip he had tossed over his shoulder. "Fine, you may stay there."

He headed out the door and off toward the lists, passing the stable along the way. The stable lad was bringing a new horse into the building.

That horse looked extremely familiar.

"Where did that horse come from?" he asked, circling back. "Have the lasses returned from the abbey?"

"The abbey?" the lad repeated, giving him an odd look. "Nay, we found this mare grazing in the meadow. No one claimed her, so Aedan said to bring her in." He gave Ruari an odd look. "Do you recognize this horse, my lord? She's a fine mare, pretty coloring. She looked lost."

Ruari rubbed the horse's flank and grinned. "I believe I

do. This horse belongs to Juliana, the lass we escorted to the abbey. She'll be happy to learn she's safe." He'd searched for the mare on his way home, to no avail.

"You're correct in that assessment," Padraig said as he joined him, coming from the lists and wiping the sweat from his brow. He tossed his sword to the ground as he approached the chestnut-colored mare. The animal lifted its head and whinnied.

Ruari crooned, "Hush, we'll not hurt you, lassie. Do you miss your rider? Lady Juliana is off to Stonecroft Abbey, though I know not how long she'll be before she returns."

"Do you think the mare brought herself back here?" Padraig asked thoughtfully. "Do you believe animals can find their way home?"

He continued to rub the horse's muzzle. "She's never been to the Cameron Keep before, but she has been around some of our horses. Mayhap she recognized a familiar scent."

Brin joined them and said, "Come on, Padraig. I need some porridge."

"Join us, Ruari?" Padraig asked as the two moved toward the keep.

"Nay, I just ate. You two go along while I calm this beautiful animal."

Padraig didn't go far before he turned around and said, "Just beware. My cousin's son has a Highland pony that seems to be possessed by a strange spirit. That pony has saved his life more than once. There was never a more devoted pet, but I'm not ashamed to say he scares me. You can never know what goes on inside a wee beastie's mind."

Brin said, "Steenie's only five. Papa said I must wait until I'm twelve summers to have a horse of my own." The lad's face fell.

Ruari ruffled the wee lad's hair. "You'll have a pet someday." He knew just how it felt to be considered too young for everything.

For anything.

He'd always been Aedan's younger brother, in his shadow. Wee Heckie squirmed slightly against his chest as if to send him a message. "Brin?" Ruari said. "I think Heckie is out of danger. Would you like to adopt him as your pet?"

The lad's face lit up with sheer delight. "You would give him to me? I'll take good care of him." He tore back to put his hands out for the puppy.

"You have to ask for your mama and papa's permission first, but if they approve, he's your pet. I know you'll take good care of him. As long as I can visit with him whenever I want." He handed the dog over to Brin, giving him one last pet on his head. Although he'd enjoyed taking care of the pup, it felt right giving him to Brin. It felt like the best way he could tell the lad that he was worthy, that he was important.

"My thanks, Uncle Ruari." He cuddled the pup under his chin, and Heckie sighed in contentment before settling in for another nap.

Ruari chuckled at the animal's antics. "As long as your parents agree."

"I promise to ask them both." Brin hurried to catch up with Padraig.

Once they were alone, Juliana's favorite horse continued to nuzzle him, but she let out a soft cry that sounded mournful. "You're missing your lady, are you not?"

The horse pushed him a bit.

"Fine, I'll take you to her," he said, his heart beating faster at the thought, "but only if you keep quiet."

The horse took in a deep breath and sighed just like Heckie had.

———◆———

Juliana crept out the back door of the kitchens, not wanting anyone to see her. She just had to get away. Joan's constant babble about the joys of being a nun—and the inevitability that Juliana would take her vows—was making her anxious.

She didn't have the heart to tell Joan that she simply wasn't interested in taking her vows. At least, not yet. Although she didn't feel drawn to being a nun, she still did not wish to marry the man her sire had chosen for her.

She stepped carefully through the brush and made her way toward the front of the abbey, moving past the stables. Wistfulness washed over her at the thought of her lost friend. Her dear horse, Winnie, was still missing. She'd hoped the animal would find her way here. She'd heard that animals' sense of smell was so strong they could often follow the people they loved.

Winnie didn't have that feeling for her, apparently. She sighed, glancing up at the full moon, her heart full of longing for Winnie. And, if she were being honest, for Ruari too. Scant clouds passed in front of the luminous object, lighting up the herb garden with an eerie glow, although it did not deter her from her wandering.

Stonecroft Abbey's garden was quite large. Full of herbs and various vegetables, it had a lovely scent unlike anything she'd ever smelled before. The back of the garden next to the curtain wall was full of fruit trees, though they were just budding. This was a perfect spot for her to clear her mind and give careful thought to what she really wanted.

She sat on the cold stone, not caring about the temperature, arranging her skirts carefully to keep herself as warm as possible. Tipping her head back, she took in the beauty of the night, the dark blue sky dotted with bright stars, occasionally covered with moving clouds.

A twig broke behind her. She bolted up, whirling around as a scream built in her throat, but her gaze caught the dark red hair of Ruari Cameron. Instead of screaming, she let out a low squeal of delight, throwing herself at him and wrapping her arms around his neck before she thought better of her boldness and stepped back.

Ruari smiled at her and said, "I wish I'd get that kind of reception from you every time we meet."

She blushed and stared at her boots, wiggling her toes against the cobblestones. "Forgive me, but I thought you were someone I didn't know and I feared the worst. I was verra pleased to see it was you. But why have you returned so soon?"

He pulled her close, his hands settling on her hips. "I came to give you good news."

Her heart raced at the contact, pounding so hard and fast she wondered if he could feel it, too.

She liked being this close to him. She *savored* it. And she was done denying her feelings. She would tell Joan in the morn exactly how she felt about this man.

"I have a surprise for you," he whispered. "I brought your horse. She returned to Cameron land so I thought…"

She didn't allow him to finish, so pleased with his news that she threw her arms around his neck and hugged him tight.

But something different happened this time.

Her heart still pounded and raced, but a strange heat coursed through her. She liked Ruari Cameron. She pulled back to stare up at him. She liked his looks, his scent, his eyes, his touch, his shoulders, his…everything.

What didn't she like?

Before she could consider that thought, his lips descended on hers, the warmth of them pressing against her. She couldn't have been more surprised. Her lips parted with a will of their own, and his tongue touched hers tentatively.

She wouldn't tell her sister how much she liked the taste of Ruari Cameron, although it was true.

She whimpered and opened her mouth. He slanted his mouth over hers, deepening their contact, and his tongue teased hers. Oh, how she wished this could go on forever.

Instead, a roar interrupted them.

"What goes on here?" the abbess shouted.

CHAPTER TEN

R UARI ENDED THE KISS ABRUPTLY and pivoted on his heel, tucking Juliana behind him. "Abbess Mary, forgive my indiscretion. This was all my fault. I came upon the lady in the garden and I took advantage of her. She is innocent of any wrongdoing."

Juliana stood on her tiptoes and peeked over his shoulder. "Nay, I'm not completely innocent. I rather enjoyed it, but do forgive me, Mother Mary." Her hands gripped his shoulder, something he rather liked, but he hoped she'd stay behind him. He didn't wish for her to get into any trouble on his account, although he was more certain than ever that she should not go through with becoming a nun.

"Lady Juliana, you will take yourself back inside the abbey while I have a word with Lord Cameron. And may I remind you that you should not have been out here in the middle of the night alone? Why have you returned, Lord Cameron? And how did you know he would be out here, lass? Oh, my heavens. Praise the Lord to give me strength. Inside, my dear. I'll speak with you and your sister soon enough, though I know not whether to wake poor Sister Joan given all she's had to contend with of late." The poor nun looked flustered, her hand going to the crucifix she always wore around her neck. The wind ruffled her long dark habit around her thin frame.

"Please, nay, wait until morn to tell her," Juliana said, still clinging to Ruari.

"Silence. You will not argue with me," the older woman said, tightening the belt around her waist. She lifted her hand from the side of her body and turned to point to the abbey. "Get yourself inside."

Juliana did as she was bid, hurrying away into the dark, casting a quick glance at Ruari over her shoulder.

It took every bit of self-control he possessed not to wink at her. Hell, he'd never wanted a lass this much before. She was both sweet *and* had spirit. But he needed to be respectful of the circumstance. It had been poor judgment on his part to kiss her outside the abbey.

"Ruari Cameron, your brother will be verra disappointed to hear you've been indiscreet with a lass on our property. I'll speak with the lass's sister, but I'll be sending her back to Lochluin Abbey on the morrow. She is clearly not a candidate to take her vows. I assume you'll stay and escort them back. May I also ask about your intentions? Shall I tell her sister you'll be offering for her as soon as you return to Cameron land?" Mother Mary crossed her arms in front of her while she awaited his response.

The words came as a shock, though they shouldn't have. And to his surprise, the notion wasn't disagreeable to him. Indeed, he rather liked the thought of taking Juliana to wife, which came as a shock given he'd vowed never to marry again. Destiny had a way of interfering with the best-laid plans.

"Offering for her?" he said softly, thinking on it, "I probably will, but I think 'tis a bit soon for that."

"I found you outside with the lass in the middle of the night with no chaperone. I found her *in your arms.* I'd be within my right if I were to insist you marry her here before you leave, but to do so would unsettle me." The abbess's foot tapped at a rapid pace, showing him the extent of her vexation.

Ruari rubbed the scruff of his whiskers, too stunned to

speak. Though lads and lasses were not forced to marry if found engaged in a simple kiss, her sire would probably view the matter differently.

"I'll consider offering for her once I speak with my brother. I'm assuming her sister will be returning with us, so I can speak with the two of them together once I've made my decision."

The abbess leaned toward him and whispered, "I'll go pray that you make the right decision, my lord." She glanced at him through narrowed lids—the kind of glance that made him want to confess to every sin he'd ever committed.

Once she left, he fell back onto the bench he and Juliana had been standing in front of when he'd kissed her.

Marriage.

He'd sworn never to marry again, simply because his first marriage had been a disaster. Doirin hadn't cared about any of the things that were important to him, and the opposite was also true.

How would it feel to be married to Juliana Clavelle?

For starters, there'd be a possibility of love because they obviously had feelings for each other. Juliana, while an innocent, had ignited in his arms, full of a passion and desire he wanted to see more of, but how could he without marriage?

He couldn't deny that his intention had been for a soft, sweet kiss, yet it had turned into something that had been anything but soft and sweet. In fact, he'd nearly mauled the poor lass, but then again, she'd matched every bit of his ardor.

While every part of his brain fought the idea of marrying again, he had to admit that the part of him that had beaten with a pulsating fury when they'd kissed wanted more. She was different than Doirin, of that he was certain.

Much as he wished to deny his feelings, he couldn't deny that he'd made the decision to bring her horse to the abbey without consulting with anyone, and he'd come alone. That much spoke volumes of his feelings for her, even if he didn't wish to acknowledge them.

He'd come alone because he was anxious to spend more time with the lass and gain her favor.

Aye, he wanted Juliana Clavelle, and he was prepared to wed her.

———————

Juliana marched back to the abbey, her steps loud enough to be overheard, but another emotion overcame her as she stood outside the door. Tears threatened to tear from her chest, and she didn't wish to awaken everyone in the abbey.

Besides, Ruari had brought her dearest Winnie back to her, and she hadn't even seen her yet.

Glancing over her shoulder, she saw the nun was deep in conversation with Ruari. Neither of them were likely to notice if she slipped off to the stables instead. Once she determined she could make the trip safely, she made a quarter turn and tiptoed until she found grass to walk on so her steps wouldn't be heard.

Mother Mary's voice carried across the land, and although part of her was tempted to listen, she went instead to the stables.

She opened the door and stepped inside. A stable lad sat up on the pallet in the corner, his eyes heavy with sleep, but she waved him back down. "I'm just here to see my horse, wherever she is. The one Ruari Cameron brought."

The lad pointed down toward the end of the stalls, so she hurried in that direction, pleased when she finally heard the soft nicker of her dear mare. "Winnie!" she said, trying her best to quiet her voice so the abbess wouldn't hear her through the walls. She fell against the chestnut beauty, wrapping her arms around the horse's neck as she finally dissolved into a flurry of tears.

What had she done?

The abbess was furious, her sister would be upset enough to send her home, and Ruari…?

She had no idea how Ruari felt. As if prompted by a question from the beast, she murmured into her soft fur, "Aye, I do like him. But what have I done?"

Her horse whinnied as if to soothe her, and Juliana felt at home for the first time in days. The sensation gave her a new sense of clarity.

She didn't belong in an abbey.

She didn't want to become a nun.

She would not take her vows.

On the morrow, she'd confess what she'd done to Joan, but she'd also tell her that sisterhood wasn't for her. Even if it meant she and Joan could not be together. "'Tis not for me at all, sweet Winnie."

Approaching footsteps caught her attention, and she swiped at the tears on her cheeks, forcing herself not to cry anymore. She hadn't done anything wrong.

Moments later, Ruari swept into the stall, his eyes full of concern. And something else. "I thought you'd gone inside, but the stable lad told me you were in here crying. I told the abbess it was all my fault. I'm sorry for taking advantage of your innocence."

Juliana continued to stare at her dear pet, her breath hitching once before she managed to say, "I'm not sorry."

Ruari reached down and placed a finger under her chin, tipping her face up gently until their eyes met. "You aren't?"

She couldn't speak, but she shook her head adamantly, locking her gaze on his.

He didn't say anything for a long moment, the two of them staring at each other.

"I don't wish to be a nun. I don't want to live in an abbey. I would prefer to marry someone I care for deeply and have his bairns. But that man is not the one my sire chose for me."

"Your sire has betrothed you to another?"

She gave a slight nod, and Ruari's hand fell from her face. She continued, lifting her chin a notch, "But I have not accepted. I don't wish to marry him. He's more than twenty years older than me. My sister doesn't wish for me to marry him either."

"May I ask his name?"

"Ailbeart Munro."

Ruari thought for a moment, then said, "I don't know him, but you should have a say in whom you marry."

"My father allowed me this visit because my sister requested it. He'll allow me to escape the marriage only if I take my vows."

"Have you met Munro?"

"Nay, I don't wish to. I've not heard anything nice of him. He's been married once already."

"There is another possibility. Will you marry me?"

Her heart started beating fast again, and emotion clogged her throat as Ruari took her hand and searched her gaze. "I know we don't know each other well, but I think we would suit. I like you verra much, and I would definitely like to court you. Mayhap we could marry at Lochluin Abbey. Your father might agree to you marrying me. I'm eight and twenty, so I am a bit older, but not twenty years."

Juliana hadn't dared to hope he might make such an offer. Marriage to Ruari would be agreeable. Nay, more than agreeable. She felt sure she could love this man. But would Joan accept her decision?

"You're thinking too hard," he said, his face falling. "I see you don't agree that we may suit."

She said, "Nay! 'Tis not so. I was thinking about Joan. I like the idea because I like you verra much. But I need to speak with my sister first. But if you truly mean it, and my sister agrees, then my answer to your question is aye."

Ruari smiled and pulled her into his arms, his embrace warm and inviting. A promise.

Winnie nickered and lifted her head as if to give her approval, something that made Juliana smile.

"I think 'tis best if you go inside. Talk with your sister on the morrow. I believe I'll be escorting you both back to Lochluin Abbey. You can give me your answer then."

Her life had taken a sudden turn for the better.

She could soon be the wife of Ruari Cameron.

CHAPTER ELEVEN

———————

JOAN WAS FEELING MUCH BETTER in the morrow, so she'd agreed to meet with the abbess after they broke their fast in the great hall. Although Joan did not say why they sat in the abbess's private chamber, Juliana certainly knew why, and her hands trembled with nerves.

Mother Mary greeted her. "Sister Joan, you look much better this morn. How are you feeling?"

"I feel much better. I'm sure I'll be tending to my usual duties in another sennight. I'll start today, but mayhap I'll only work for half the day."

Mother Mary folded her hands in her lap as she leaned back from her desk. "Has Juliana informed you of her activities last eve?"

Joan glanced at Juliana, confused. "Nay. What transpired last eve?" Her sister's face lost color, something that caused Juliana to start twisting her gown in her hands. Poor Joan had just gotten back on her feet. Would her transgression send her back to her sickbed?

Mother Mary nodded to Juliana, indicating it was her turn to explain everything. She'd hoped the abbess would speak for her, but she'd prepared herself for this possibility. Indeed, she hadn't slept much last night—instead lying awake and planning what she'd say.

Juliana cleared her throat, blushed, and said to her sister, "I went for a walk after dark because I was confused about my calling. I'm just not sure if I am meant to take my vows…"

The abbess noticeably cleared her throat, so Juliana moved on to the critical part of her tale. "I encountered Ruari Cameron. Winnie had found her way back to Cameron land, and he immediately brought her to me because he knows how dear she is to me."

"Juliana!" Mother Mary prodded. "Your feelings about an animal are not part of this discussion!"

She did her best to ignore the fact that an abbess was yelling at her. "He found me in the herb garden and we… well…he kissed me and…"

Juliana didn't have the chance to finish the tale because her sister shot out of her seat, her face now livid.

"How could you? And you saw them, Mother Mary? You've embarrassed yourself and me? I don't know what else to say except to repeat myself. How *could* you?"

Everyone was always trying to control her, from her sire to her sister, and she was sick of it. She decided to speak what was in her heart, even though both listeners in front of her would probably disagree with her. "Joan, I don't think I wish to take my vows. I don't think I am interested in becoming a nun. I would like…"

"You would rather marry someone like Ailbeart Munro, who will abuse you and treat you as if you have little value more than a mouse running through the fields? I see I'll have to tell you all that marriage involves so you'll finally understand why you won't enjoy it. Men paw you and take you as they wish. They…"

The abbess stood, her cheeks flaming red. "Sister Joan! You will hold those thoughts to yourself and not repeat them in my abbey. You will take your leave now, go to chapel, and pray for forgiveness for speaking such horrific remarks in front of me. Go now!" She pointed toward the door. Her thin frame shook visibly underneath the voluminous robes of her habit. Juliana prayed she wouldn't crumple to the ground. She was partially at fault for upsetting the older woman.

The rebuke rendered Joan speechless for a moment. She stood staring at the abbess, her mouth slightly open, then finally said, "But everything I say is true. She has a right to know the truth, and 'tis my responsibility to tell her since we lost our mother."

"Go now!" The two-word command came out in an angry bellow.

Joan left hastily.

Once she left, the abbess took a seat again. "You will disregard all your sister said. You will return to Lochluin Abbey. I have already dispatched a messenger to your sire's residence so he is aware of your transgression."

A lump formed in Juliana's throat that she fought to force back down. "My father?" How would he react? Would he insist that she return home at once to wed his choice of husband?

"Your sister will return with you. I have discussed the issue with Ruari Cameron, and I expect he will offer for you as he should."

Juliana's hands gripped the arms of the chair she sat in. "You? *You* told him to offer for me?"

"Of course. He was found mishandling you. A man does not kiss an innocent lass unless he plans to marry her. A bairn could be just around the corner. I'm sure your sire will see it the same way."

A bairn? From kissing? That was not what the serving lasses had told her. They'd told her about the man and the woman...something she didn't wish to think about. But it was far more than kissing. Private parts, pushing, moaning, those were all the things she'd heard. How she wished her sister had explained it all to her.

Would she ever learn the truth?

Ruari had moaned when they'd kissed...as had she. Could it be?

No, she refused to believe such drivel. Kissing would not create a new life. Then her mind came back to the part that truly hurt her the most.

"You told him he should marry me?"

"Of course. 'Tis only right, though I told him it could wait until you return to Lochluin Abbey."

Juliana ran from the chamber, tears flooding her face.

Ruari didn't wish to marry her at all. He'd been forced into it.

———

They'd nearly reached Cameron land, and Ruari still hadn't had the opportunity to speak with Juliana. While her sister guarded her like a chieftain, he'd expected she would slip away to speak with him during the short break they took, but she'd avoided making eye contact.

He would have to take matters into his own hands. And so, before they reached the abbey, Ruari approached Joan's horse first and said, "I request a brief moment of your time before you return to the abbey, Sister Joan. And I'd appreciate it if you'd allow Juliana to join us."

Sister Joan gave him a terse glare but nodded.

Ruari pointed to an area outside the stables, then gave instructions to the guards who'd traveled with them, sending some back to Stonecroft Abbey. Others would stay at Lochluin.

He found his way over to the area he'd chosen for their conversation, a small clearing, and waited until Sister Joan and Juliana joined him. "Sister Joan," he said, nodding to her before greeting her sister. "Juliana." Again she refused to make eye contact with him, her gaze solidly on the ground in front of her feet.

Nevertheless, he continued, "Sister, I'd like to apologize for my indiscretion. I should have asked for permission to court Juliana properly instead of taking advantage of her innocence."

"Aye, you did, Lord Cameron, and you're to keep your distance from her. She is not interested in you."

Ruari wasn't sure what to say to that, but he forged ahead with the words he'd planned. "I'd like to ask for Juliana's hand in marriage. I would have preferred to court her to be certain we suit, but under the circumstances..." He paused because Juliana burst into tears. He wasn't sure how to react to that, but he finished his sentence. "Under the circumstances, mayhap we should marry sooner. I meant no disrespect to either of you. I have strong feelings for her..."

Sister Joan held her hand up. "Stop right there. You need not continue with your lies. We know the abbess told you to offer for her. Juliana is confused and does not wish to take her vows, so we've been sent away. She has been shamed, and our sire has arranged for her immediate marriage. He is on his way here. She'll be married to her betrothed within a sennight."

Ruari was stunned. "But I'd like to marry her myself."

Juliana sobbed even harder. He wished to console her, wrap his arms around her, but her sister stood in front of her, guarding her like any bear protecting its youngest cub.

He peeked around Sister Joan and asked, "Juliana? Why do you cry so?"

No one answered his question.

"I'd like to request a private word with your sister," he said to Sister Joan. "Two minutes under that tree there, where you can see us."

"Nay, you'll not speak to her again. You've broken her heart and shamed her, Lord Cameron. I'll not allow you to hurt her again. Please leave us."

The hell with her sister. "Juliana, please," he said, seeking her out with his eyes. "I *must* speak with you."

To his surprise, she pushed her sister aside and stepped forward. "Just answer me one question, Ruari Cameron."

"Anything. What is it?"

"Did the abbess tell you it was your duty to marry me?" Ruari was rendered speechless. He didn't know how to answer her honestly without her thinking the worst of him.

"You have your answer, Juliana." Her sister grabbed her hand and tugged on her.

Ruari said, "Aye, she did, Juliana, but I would have asked you on my own. Why do you think I brought your horse back to you without any guards? I was interested in you and couldn't wait to see you again."

She glanced back at him over her shoulder, tears streaming down her face, but she said nothing.

Ruari's world fell apart.

He'd thought the only thing he cared about was becoming his brother's second.

But failing at this felt so much worse.

CHAPTER TWELVE

———◆———

R UARI STEPPED INTO HIS BROTHER'S solar, closing the door behind him just before Aedan exploded. "A nun! You've shamed a nun? What were you thinking? You've been telling me you'll never marry again. 'Twas all a big mistake, yet you were nearly caught with your hands up a nun's skirts!"

"Aedan, you have it all wrong. I...we...I kissed her and the abbess caught us. But I wish to court her. It happened much faster than I ever imagined, but I have strong feelings for her. She's not a nun yet, and she has decided not to take her vows. I believe we would suit."

"The hell you suit. You'll stay the hell away from her. I will not allow you to shame the Cameron name in such a way. You'll stay away from the abbey for at least a fortnight."

Ruari didn't know exactly what to do, but he couldn't let this go. "Aedan, I offered for her. Her sister rejected me, but I heard her sire is on his way, and I plan to ask for her hand in marriage when he arrives."

Aedan stood behind his desk, both hands braced on the top. "Ruari, what is wrong with you?" he asked. His voice sounded calm, but Ruari knew better. This was always how Aedan sounded before his anger turned into a raging fury.

Perhaps it would be better if he gave him time to process everything before pressing his suit. "Aedan, she has chosen not to take her vows."

"Because of you?" He leaned forward, his eyes bulging from their sockets. When had he last seen Aedan this upset? "Nay, she's not interested in becoming a nun. I don't think she ever was. She's young and confused. I believe her sister is the one who wants her to be a nun."

Aedan sat down behind his desk, then ran his hand through his thick brown locks now peppered with gray strands.

The door opened and Jennie stepped inside, closing the door behind her quietly. She leaned against it as if to physically block either of them from leaving. "Aedan, I don't like it when you allow your temper to control your actions. 'Tis not good for your body."

Aedan motioned for his wife to come closer. "Jennie, you take over. I don't know what to do with him. Mother Mary from Stonecroft sent me a message stating my brother was inappropriate with one of their novices. What am I to think? You know we must protect and respect the abbey. 'Tis Clan Cameron's sacred responsibility. Saints above, he's acting like a love-sick fool. You cannot go about kissing lasses who are thinking of taking their vows, Ruari. I hear her sire is on his way here because he's furious."

Jennie's mouth had formed a little 'oh' of surprise, but she shook it off quickly. "If he is, we'll handle it," she said quickly.

Aedan stared at his wife. "What can I possibly tell him to explain my brother's behavior? He's nearly a decade older than the lass."

Jennie turned to Ruari, giving him a reassuring half smile, and shrugged her shoulders. "Tell me what your thoughts were, please?" She moved over behind her husband and placed her hands on his shoulders. "Aedan, please remember that your brother is a man grown, and 'tis not unusual at all for a couple to have a difference in age."

From the hall came a screech. "Aedan! Aedan!"

Aedan hastened to the door and opened it. "What is it,

Mother?"

"Must you yell so? I'm sure Ruari has his reasons for whatever he's done. Listen to your brother, my dear." He could see over Aedan's shoulder that their mother sat a good distance from them, in front of the hearth in the great hall. Which meant plenty of other people had likely overheard them, too.

"We're fine, Mama. Do not concern yourself with us," Aedan ground out through clenched teeth before he closed the door quietly. "Jennie, talk to him. He's being incredibly dense."

"Go ahead, Ruari," she said gently. "Tell me your thoughts."

Ruari took a deep breath and explained, "I have verra strong feelings for her…" He hesitated to say his next thought, but he needed Aedan to understand. "My feelings for her are already much stronger than what I felt for Doirin." He cast his gaze downward, embarrassed to admit such a thing.

"You were too young to marry," Jennie said. "It was pushed upon you. I don't blame you for anything that happened with Doirin. You know that. You were ill-suited for each other."

Aedan said, "It could have worked. We did not know they were ill-suited when they married."

Jennie said, "Husband, you're not helping. You pushed that marriage on him as much as Doirin and her sire did. It didn't work. Aye, he was a fine member of our clan, but it didn't work. Most of us knew that Doirin had other interests in this relationship. She wished to go to court and be on display, not carry bairns. She wished to be dressed in jewels and silks. That is not your brother, nor is it you. 'Tis over and forgotten."

"I'll never forget what happened, Jennie," Ruari whispered, his heart heavy with pain.

"I know, Ruari. None of us will forget Doirin. But that

doesn't mean you can't marry again. Now tell me about Juliana."

"I like her verra much. I wish to court her." He did his best to ignore his brother, focusing on Jennie, someone he trusted to be calm and reasonable. Someone he trusted to listen to him.

"And how do you know that?" his brother asked.

"Know what?" He glanced from Jennie to Aedan, confused.

"How do you know you like her, Ruari? You've hardly spent any time with her," Aedan bellowed again, but he visibly calmed when Jennie squeezed his shoulders.

"Padraig and I spoke with her on the way to Lochluin Abbey. I talked with her quite a bit when we escorted her to Stonecroft Abbey, and I enjoyed our conversation verra much. You'll recall that I protected her from the reiver attack near the abbey. I consoled her, but I know how much the violence had shaken her, even more so the loss of her horse. When the horse was found on Cameron land, I knew I must return her horse to her at once. 'Tis why I went back."

"Without an escort." Aedan glared at his brother, his arms now crossed in front of him.

"Aye, without an escort."

"Why?"

"Because I didn't wish to wait," he said, knowing it was a weak reason, but it was better than admitting the lass had addled his mind.

"Or is it possible you were not thinking straight because thoughts of the lass have clouded your mind?" Jennie asked.

Leave it to the healer to see the truth in someone's heart. Forcing himself to look Jennie in the eye, he squared his shoulders. "Aye. 'Struth. I cannot stop thinking about her. And I surely was not thinking when I found her in the herb garden, told her about her mare, and kissed her."

Aedan bolted out of his chair, throwing his arms over

his head. "This is what I mean. Had you no thought in your mind that you were outside an abbey? That she was thinking of taking her vows?"

"Nay, 'twas not like that at all," he shouted back at his brother, tired of the thick judgment in his tone. "I told her about her horse, she threw her arms around my neck, and the kiss just happened."

"Nay, you took advantage of a vulnerable lass."

"Nay, the abbess caught us, so I proposed. I wanted to court her, and this pushed up the wedding, but Aedan, I probably would have fallen in love with her anyway."

Jennie turned to her husband, her hands on her hips. "Took advantage? Aedan, may I take a moment to remind you of our first time together on the hill directly behind the abbey?"

To Ruari's surprise, Aedan burst into a huge smile and leaned over to kiss his wife's cheek. "I'll never forget that night."

Jennie arched her brow at her husband, whose expression quickly reverted to a scowl. She then returned to Ruari. "You think you love her?" Jennie asked. Her mouth tipped up at the corners, just slightly, as if she didn't wish Aedan to guess she was smiling.

Ruari thought for a moment, then said, "I think so. Or at least I think I will love her. She's given me hope, something I haven't felt in a long time. I don't have many positive experiences with women, if you recall. This friendship has been wonderful for me."

"Friendship?" Aedan asked.

"Aye, friendship. 'Tis how it started. Whether or not you support me, I intend to ask her sire for her hand. As I said, I tried speaking with her sister, but she was not willing to consider my suit."

"What does Juliana want?" Jennie asked.

"She told me she would marry me if her sister agreed."

"But her sister disagreed," Aedan said.

"Aye, and I think she's turned Juliana against me. I wish to speak to her alone."

"Ruari, all right. I'll accept you have feelings for her and wish to do the right thing, but you must tread verra carefully. Please do not anger the abbesses."

Ruari didn't care to listen to his brother any longer. Although he could remind him that Juliana didn't want to take her vows, he knew it wouldn't help. Why did his own brother continue to think the worst of him? Jennie believed in him, and for now, that would have to be enough. He spun on his heel and stalked out of his brother's solar.

There was no point telling Aedan what was in his heart. He would not give up in his pursuit of Juliana Clavelle.

Nay, he would marry the woman who'd given him hope.

CHAPTER THIRTEEN

—◆—

JULIANA SAT INSIDE THE ABBESS'S solar with Mother Matilda and her sister. How she wished she had her needlework to keep her hands busy. She did her best to stop squirming in her seat, but she failed miserably.

"Sister Joan," the abbess said. "I believe you must accept the fact that your sister is no longer interested in becoming a nun. I don't think, in view of the situation, that it would be appropriate for her to continue." Juliana was pleased that this abbess did not seem as upset or angry about the circumstances as the abbess at Stonecroft Abbey.

"Please, Mother Matilda. She does not wish to marry. Allow her to become a novice."

The abbess looked at Juliana and tilted her head. "Juliana? What say you about marriage? From what I was told, Lord Cameron has offered for you as has another person, who is coming to visit you along with your sire."

Juliana glanced from the abbess to her sister. She'd known her sire was coming, but she hadn't expected him to bring her betrothed.

"Munro? Is he bringing Ailbeart Munro?" her sister asked, her eyes wide with shock.

"I know not who he is bringing, but there is a man traveling with him and both of them would like to meet with Juliana. Think you this will be a problem?" the abbess asked calmly.

Her tone did nothing to calm the beating of her own heart or her sister's.

"She'll not see him," Joan declared, crossing her arms.

Juliana fought back tears because she truly did not know how to handle any of this. Her world had descended into chaos from one kiss. If Ruari had offered for her on his own free will, she would have been overjoyed to marry him. But he'd been coerced, and she'd just learned that her sire was bringing another man for her to marry.

She was back to where she'd been when she first arrived at the abbey.

Her sire wished for her to marry a stranger.

Her dearest sister wished for her to be a nun.

Neither of them had asked what she wanted, and she didn't rightly know. "I'm not sure, Mother Matilda."

"Did you agree to marry Ruari Cameron? He says you did."

Her sister turned to glare at her. "Nay, she did not."

Juliana corrected her. "Aye, I did, but I'm confused."

"You cannot marry a Cameron," her sister insisted. She'd repeated this time and again over the last day.

Mother Matilda folded her hands on the desk and leaned toward Joan. "Why not? I think 'twould be a wonderful match for her. I've known the Cameron lads all my life and they are as honorable as any men I've ever met. What have you against Ruari Cameron?"

Her sister squirmed in her seat, uncomfortable now that the questioning had been shifted to her. Juliana was tempted to defend her sister, but in truth, she wished to hear her answer.

"I just don't believe they would suit," Joan replied, lifting her chin a notch.

"So you'd prefer for her to marry the stranger whom your sire is bringing along?" Juliana thought she saw a wee bit of humor behind the abbess's smile. Something about this woman appealed to her on a deep level. She sensed she would be nothing if not fair. Mother Mathilda leaned back in her chair with one hand rested on the desk.

"Nay! She's not to marry!"

"Sister Joan, is your objection due to your personal feelings about men, or Juliana's feelings? Because if you are passing your feelings on to your sister, I don't think 'tis fair to her."

Joan's eyes misted and she swiped at one tear that had formed. "I don't want her hurt."

"Many women marry and are verra happy. Do you think Jennie Cameron is unhappy? You've had many dealings with her over the years."

Joan squeezed her eyes shut and shook her head. "Nay, Mother Matilda. I believe she is happy."

The abbess turned to Juliana, leaning toward her. "Is your heart set against marriage, child?"

Juliana stared at her hands. "Nay, I cannot say it is. I think it would please me to find a man to love and marry him. I thought Ruari could be that person and I accepted his suit, but only if Joan agreed." She didn't admit that he'd confessed to being prompted by Mother Mary to offer for her. That hurt too much to even say. Although he'd claimed he would have offered for her anyway, how could she ever know if that were true?

"And I do *not* agree."

The abbess leaned back in her chair and folded her hands in her lap. "Sister Joan, I'm going to send you off to have a conversation with our Lord. You are to search your soul for the answer to this question: Are you doing what you think is in the best interest of your sister or in your own best interest?"

Emotion flashed through Joan's eyes, then she got up and fled the solar, leaving Juliana more confused than ever.

———◆———

Ruari stood outside the gates of the abbey with Padraig.

"Are you sure you wish to do this, cousin?" the younger man asked.

Ruari glanced up at the sky as the sun dipped lower on the horizon. "Aye, I do. If the abbess will allow it, I'd like to speak to her sister, see if I can convince her that Juliana and I will suit. Once their sire arrives, I'll ask for an audience with him. I don't want her marrying another."

"Are you truly ready to declare for her?" Padraig asked, tipping his head with a wry grin. "This isn't just pride?"

"Nay. I do have strong feelings for her. I think I do love her, but I'm not sure I know what love is."

"Many say when you find the one, you'll know. Instinct," Padraig said as he patted the center of his chest. "Right here, you'll know it."

"Then she's the one. I admit I've never felt this way about another lass. I don't wish to lose her."

Padraig clasped his shoulder. "Then I'll send good wishes with you as you speak to the abbess. I'll await your news right here." He found a few blades of grass to chew on and leaned up against a big oak tree.

Ruari took a deep breath, moved to the entrance, and stepped into the area just inside the door. He told himself this would be much different than the situation at Stonecroft Abbey. To Mother Mary, he was no better than a passing rogue trying to get underneath a lass's skirts, but the people of Lochluin Abbey knew him. They wouldn't automatically think the worst of his intentions.

To his relief, Sister Grace greeted him immediately. She'd visited the keep many times to read to the children, and he'd always admired her sunny disposition.

"My lord Cameron. How lovely to see you. What can I do for you today?"

"Greetings, Sister Grace. I'd like to speak with Mother Matilda for a moment."

Sister Grace giggled and covered her mouth. "I thought you were here to see Juliana. She's such a sweet lass, is she not?"

He relaxed, his self-confidence restored. She clearly approved, to some level, of his courtship of Juliana.

"She is that and more, but I'm here to see the abbess, if you please." He swallowed, trying to maintain the confidence to say everything that needed saying.

The nun disappeared for a few moments then returned rather quickly. "She said to come right along. She was hoping you'd stop to see her."

Ruari followed Sister Grace down the passageway to the abbess's chamber. She bid him to sit, and once he settled into a chair across from her desk, she didn't hesitate to speak. "Your purpose, Lord Cameron?" Mother Matilda's keen eyes settled on him.

He was more than familiar with the abbess, having spent a fair amount of time at the abbey over the years. Sometimes he escorted Jennie or Tara here to tend to the sick, and on several occasions he'd personally assisted the monks with various repairs to the building. On other trips, he'd brought the devout extra vegetables from the garden or baked goods from the kitchens. Never, as far as he knew, had he given Mother Mathilda a reason to think ill of him. She had a quick mind and a compassionate heart. He was hoping that her heart would be open to him.

"I'm here to offer for Juliana Clavelle. I'd like to make her my wife, but I understand her sister objects to the match."

The abbess took his measure for a moment, readjusted herself in her seat, then leaned forward. "Tell me about your first marriage, Ruari. Although I was present at your wedding, of course, I rarely saw you and Doirin together. Were you happy?"

Leave it to her to cut straight to the point. No more lies, he vowed to himself. It was time to face his past so he could finally put it behind him. "Nay, we were not. We wanted different things. She wished to go to court." He wasn't sure how to explain the rest.

"And what are you looking for in a marriage?" Her gaze locked on him as she awaited his answer.

"I wish for a happy life on Cameron land. And I have always wanted bairns."

"Lads or lasses?"

"I care not. I love my nieces and nephew equally."

"And you are in love with the lass?"

He'd expected her to ask, but the question still flustered him. He did his best to share the full truth as he saw it. "I cannot say for certes yet, but I have verra strong feelings for the lady. I'd like to have her by my side forever. I think we would suit. Word has reached us that her sire is coming to see her, and I heard he might be bringing the man he'd like to see her marry. I'd like to convince him to accept my offer instead, and I'm hoping you will support me in this endeavor. I thought to speak with Sister Joan, also."

Mother Mathilda nodded slightly and something inside him released. "Ruari, you have my support as I know you to be a fine, honorable man. I would like to see you happily married. Her sister is not feeling well at present. I would not recommend speaking with her. She's still hoping for Juliana to take her vows, although I suspect the lass would not be a good fit for the church. I would suggest you put all your efforts into asking her sire. He should arrive midday on the morrow." She stood, indicating their conversation had come to an end.

He stood, gave a small bow, and murmured, "My thanks to you, Mother Matilda."

She said, "I wish for you to find as much happiness as your brother has found with Jennie."

He smiled at the sentiment and left, heading down the stone passageway. It struck him that while the silence in the abbey had felt constricting when he was young, he now found it welcoming.

He stepped into the brisk night air, reveling in the smell of the fresh earth around them, the trees whistling in the wind.

Padraig was leaning against the tree, still chewing on his stalks of grass. "Are you pleased?"

"I suppose."

Padraig stood up straight and quirked an eyebrow at him.

"Mother Matilda supports my offer, but she suggested that I speak with her sire rather than her sister. They'll arrive on the morrow."

"Question for you," Padraig said, and it struck him that the lad had been thinking on this the entire time he'd been in the abbey. "Which would be more important for you—marrying Juliana or becoming your brother's second?"

Hellfire. That was a difficult question, yet he knew the answer. Still, he found he wasn't ready to admit to it. "I don't really know," he hedged.

Padraig drawled, "Then mayhap you are not ready to ask for her hand yet."

"'Tis not a fair question," Ruari said in a quick retort, lowering his voice once he realized he'd raised it.

"Why does it matter if you're Aedan's second?'

Ruari scuffed his boot in the dirt and paced a bit before he replied. "Mayhap 'tis all about Aedan's choices. He's furious with me, and I fear he'd sooner give the job to someone else." He wouldn't tell Padraig he feared the job would go to him. If it did, he'd try to be happy for his cousin.

Padraig shrugged. "I think you'd be happier with a beautiful wife in your arms than being your brother's second."

Why couldn't he have both?

CHAPTER FOURTEEN

J ULIANA CHEWED ON A FINGERNAIL, hating the
terrible habit, but unable to stop it since she was to
meet the man her sire wished for her to marry in less than
an hour. "How do I look, Joan? Do you like this gown on
me?"

"You look lovely," Joan said without looking. "I'm going
to fetch us some food from the kitchens. I shall return
shortly." She left, closing the door behind her.

Her sister hadn't said much else to her about marriage,
instead choosing to speak of other things. They'd worked
on her tapestry together, Joan exclaiming over how much
her talent had developed, and spent time on her studies.
Juliana desperately wished to learn how to read, so this
endeavor pleased her immensely.

She'd shied away from the topics of men, marriage, and
making bairns as much as Joan had. It brought out the worst
in her sister, and she wished to enjoy their relationship.

They didn't have much time left.

Juliana wore a dark gold gown that set off her light brown
locks just right. She smoothed the skirts, afraid she would
wrinkle them. Nerves raced through her, and she started
pacing back and forth in the small chamber before she
decided perhaps it would be best if she simply sat down
and worked on her needlework. If she did, perhaps she
could figure out what was missing from the piece. But that

thought left her mind as quickly as it entered it. She had more important things on which to focus.

She'd lain awake most of the night, thinking of Ruari. How he'd made her feel. How wonderful it had felt being wrapped in his arms. How she'd loved their first kiss. And how much she'd wanted more of him…until…

The abbess of Stonecroft Abbey had interfered and *made* him promise to marry her. Well, perhaps "made" was too strong a word. It could be that she'd *convinced* him to marry her.

Only that word didn't settle with her any better than the first. Promised, convinced, forced. Each of those were too strong. Each conveyed the idea that Ruari hadn't intended to offer for her at all.

Was there a different way to approach it?

Encouraged? No.

Compelled? No.

Ordered? Absolutely not.

Suggested? Perhaps.

Her heart yearned to believe the handsome Highlander had come up with the idea on his own. That he loved her, or at least thought he could. That they could be truly happy together.

She knew it didn't matter, that her sire would likely compel her to marry Ailbeart Munro, but she couldn't stop thinking about Ruari. Mayhap she should just be grateful for the experience he'd given her? She knew how good it could feel to be close to a man, especially if that man was handsome, kind, and good, as she knew Ruari to be.

For all she knew, she might like kissing Ailbeart even *more* than she liked kissing Ruari. It seemed impossible, but if it happened, she'd know right away that it was meant to be.

Something about the idea sent her pulse to racing. What if she and Ailbeart were meant for each other? He'd wanted to marry her all along, and no one had coerced him into it. Mayhap such a test was just what she needed to read her heart.

Her sister returned with a tray of food. This time she did look at Juliana, and she heaved a defeated sigh. "Juliana, you look lovely, too lovely. I'd prefer you be dressed in a dreadful garment that hung loosely on you, hiding your womanly curves."

She set down her needlework and frowned at her sister. "But why?"

"Because then Laird Munro wouldn't be interested in you," she said, avoiding eye contact.

"That would prove he's rather shallow, would it not?" Juliana asked, folding her hands in her lap.

"Aye, it would be a testament to his true character. I hope you'll see that part of him."

"You don't wish for me to marry Ailbeart Munro, do you?" Juliana asked, refusing to ignore her sister's attitude toward the possible match.

"Nay, it would not be my first preference for you. I can tell you're confused about what you want, just as I was at your age. You talked so strongly about Ruari, now you're eager to meet Ailbeart. We shall wait and see. I think his character will stand out to you. I must trust in your feelings more." She leaned down and hugged her. "I just wish the best for you, and I forget that you've grown and can think for yourself. The abbess is correct. Ruari Cameron is an honorable man, and if you choose to marry, he would indeed be an admirable choice."

She hugged Joan back, then pulled away. "Aye, you have the right of it. I don't know what I want. I'll think on it after I meet Laird Munro. I suppose it would be nice to be married to a laird."

"I must say your needlework is lovely. Tell me again why you chose this design?" Joan asked, tipping her head to get a better look at the tapestry.

"The image came to me in my dreams one night. 'Tis

a meadow full of lavender in full bloom. I've not seen one like it before, but I'm hoping it will be in my future someday soon. I'm making it for my new home, wherever 'tis."

"Juliana, 'tis most lovely," Joan said, her eyes shining. "I hope 'twill be in your future."

"Do you think Laird Munro's land looks like this? Could it be a sign of my new home? 'Tis missing something, but I cannot deduce what it might be. Mayhap it is meant to be a rendering of my husband's castle." It would be so easy if someone could tell her the right answer. If, perhaps, the wall hanging depicted the meadow leading to Munro land. Then she would know what was right for certes. Then she'd know she wasn't making a horrible mistake.

Except the thought of marrying Laird Munro made her heart feel as if it were being split in two. Did she really wish to marry Ruari? Was that the source of the conflict between her mind and heart?

Sister Grace appeared in the doorway and said, "Your sire is here and would like to see you both. The abbess has arranged for you to have the hall just to yourselves for a short time. She's ordering a small repast for your guests."

Juliana stood, hardly able to believe the moment was upon them. She stood up, smoothed her skirts for the hundredth time, pinched her cheeks for color, and stepped into the passageway, her sister behind her.

"You need not do that," Joan said in a small voice.

"Do what?" she stared at her sister, awaiting her explanation.

"Pinch your cheeks. A man shouldn't decide whether or not they like you based on your appearance." She stepped ahead of Juliana, taking the lead into the hall.

"What else do they have to base their decision upon?" Juliana asked, puzzled at her comment. Of course, a chieftain's wife must be beautiful.

Mustn't she?

They entered the hall so she never received an answer to her question. Their sire called out to them and they hastened to greet him.

But then her eyes landed on Ailbeart Munro.

He was more than handsome, he was dashing. He wore his dress plaid, shades of gray, black, and green, over a white leine. His hair was a light brown, with a beard to match, though he kept it short. He had a smile that didn't reach his eyes, but it struck her that he was staring at her with fixed interest.

This handsome man had eyes only for her.

She curtsied to him as they neared the table where the two men had been seated, then she and Joan both greeted their sire.

"My, but you are a beauty, my lady," Laird Munro said. "When have I ever seen a lass as lovely as you?"

The way he said it, so precise and sure of himself, caught her by surprise.

He gave her a slight bow. "I'm sure your sire has told you that I wish to make you my wife, Lady Juliana. Now I'm certain you'll suit me just fine. May we set a date for a sennight from now in my castle? 'Twould be most appropriate because you'll be lady of the Munro keep, so why not marry there?"

Juliana glanced at her sire and sister, not knowing how to answer. Her sister moved her to a chair and settled her while the men sat back down.

Her sister wasn't ready to sit yet. "And how many wives would Juliana make for you, Ailbeart?"

Juliana nearly flinched at the sound of his given name from her sister's lips.

"Laird to you, Sister Joan. And she will be my second and last wife. As a nun, it should be none of your affair." His voice dropped to a menacing tone that made her flinch.

Juliana couldn't help but look to her sister, waiting for her reaction.

"*Ailbeart*," Joan ground out. "My sister will not choose to be your wife, you can be certain of it, so go home."

Their sire's face turned a surprising shade of red. "Joan, you will keep your thoughts to yourself," he bellowed. "I have brought Laird Munro here to see if the two suit. This is *not* your affair. What has possessed you to speak in such a crude manner?"

Joan spun on her heel and stalked out of the great hall without another word.

Why did her sister dislike Ailbeart Munro so much?

Ruari paced outside, wishing Juliana's sire would hurry. The abbess had agreed to arrange a meeting with Clavelle near the stables of the abbey.

The man appeared out of nowhere, his hands on his hips as he stared at Ruari. "Do I know you? The abbess said someone out here wished to speak with me."

Ruari greeted him. "Nay, you do not. My brother is the chieftain of Clan Cameron. I met your daughter, Juliana, when she arrived here. We got to know each other when I escorted her to Stonecroft Abbey and back." He paused to clear his throat. "I would like to request her hand in marriage." He'd worn his best plaid and leine for the man, although he feared it would not make enough of an impression.

"Are you certain you're speaking of Juliana? She just arrived here. That would be impossible."

"Aye, I do speak of Juliana. I'm certain we would suit if..."

"Nay," the man barked. He was a tall man, though his shoulders had rounded a touch. He had probably been a fit man at one time, but life had drained him of his stamina.

"I think it would be a good match. I'm an honorable man..."

"I said nay. Leave off." He glared at Ruari as he said it,

making his meaning quite clear.

"I think we would suit. We…"

"I said nay. She is betrothed to Ailbeart Munro. They'll be married in a sennight. She's taken." He whirled around like a dancer full of too many ales and headed back inside.

Ruari wasn't going to give up. "Did she agree to this?"

He turned around and said, "She doesn't get a say. She'll do as she's told. I forbid you to see her again. Stay away."

Forbid him?

The hell with Clavelle. He would see Juliana again.

He could wager on that fact.

CHAPTER FIFTEEN

———————

JULIANA TURNED HER HEAD TO glance at her escort, the chief of Clan Munro, Ailbeart Munro. He'd offered to bring her to a nearby festival that took place once a moon in spring and summer no more than an hour's ride from the abbey. She'd accepted the offer. Munro and her father had arrived at the abbey two days ago, but she'd barely spoken with the laird after their first meeting in the hall. This was her chance to get to know him better.

Although her heart still belonged to Ruari Cameron, she had to prepare herself for the possibility that her sire might force her to marry Munro. He'd proven quite stubborn on the subject over the past two days.

Her sister was equally adamant that she should *not* marry the laird.

The two had apparently reached an impasse because her sire and her sister were no longer speaking. Joan still hadn't explained why she disapproved of Ailbeart Munro, other than his age. True, he had many gray hairs, but since his hair was so light, they didn't show much. Neither did the fine lines on his face.

Juliana preferred Ruari Cameron's rugged good looks, but no one had asked her. Nor were they likely to do so.

Munro leaned in closer and whispered in her ear, "Which side will win? The red plaids or the blue?"

She perused the mass of men tugging on opposite ends

of a very long rope, trying to decide which team appeared stronger. She thought the blue group appeared much stronger, the seven men tugging on the rope so hard the red group had to fight to keep from crossing the mark on the ground between them. "I think the blue. They're much stronger than the other group. I've never seen such an activity."

She laughed, a nervous sound, and Ailbeart leaned down and whispered, "I love the sound of your laughter. I promise you'll do it often as my wife."

The red team suddenly collapsed, the rope flying out of their hands as many of them toppled to the ground cursing. Her eyes widened at some of the expressions she heard.

"Festivals can be quite raw. My apologies that those men have no sense of honor in their comportment around ladies. What else would you like to see? Mayhap I shall purchase a gift for you," he said, his mouth stretching into a wide smile as he led her toward the colorful tents at the center of the festival.

Juliana had never witnessed such a spectacle, and she had to admit, it was magnificent. Her sire had been quite protective, only allowing her on occasion to fetch food from the vendors at the small festival occasionally held near their home. "What do they have?"

"You shall see."

The clouds kept the sun away, so it was mostly gray, but it had not yet rained. She feared ruining her only pair of good slippers. She had a sturdy pair of boots but only one pair of slippers, and both showed wear. Fortunately, her skirts kept them mostly hidden.

Ailbeart led her to the first of the booths and she gasped at the wide array of colorful hair ribbons. "Oh, how lovely."

"Naught is too good for you. Choose two of your favorites and I'll have them wrapped in twine for you to take home."

How did one properly thank a man for such a gift?

She chose a deep green velvet ribbon, plus a purple one the color of the lavender in her tapestry, both dark enough to show against her light brown hair. Thanking him graciously, she blushed when he said, "Mayhap I'll steal a kiss later as proper thanks."

She didn't know how to respond to such a comment, so she kept quiet.

"Or mayhap right now," he said, his lips meeting hers in a quick, crushing kiss that lasted only a second, but it had been long enough to tell her one thing.

She didn't like it. It was nothing like Ruari Cameron's kiss.

Her heart sunk in her chest. Part of her had hoped she'd fall in love with Ailbeart—it would have been so much easier that way. But she tried to ignore the sensation and enjoy herself. She could decide what to do later.

Ailbeart led her past the next booth, full of daggers and other small weaponry, and on to the one next to it. "This is my gift to you. Choose a pair to match each ribbon."

Juliana gasped at the array of beautiful beaded slippers in front of her. They had every color of the rainbow! She fell in love with a golden pair, and even though they weren't purple or green, she still chose that pair. After searching the others, her gaze fell on a dark purple pair with forest green beads on it. She pointed to that pair, and Ailbeart announced, "Only the best for my betrothed."

He said it loudly, confidently, and his voice carried. Except Juliana hadn't agreed to marry him yet.

Then again, he hadn't asked. Her sire hadn't said anything to her yet. Was her destiny to be decided so easily? Should she deny him here in front of others? Somehow, she knew that wouldn't be a wise choice, so she kept it to herself. Surely they could discuss the issue later, at the abbey. Surely she still had a chance to wed Ruari if she so chose.

She gasped as someone familiar stepped up to her.

Someone who seemed to have stepped right out of her thoughts.

Ruari wore a brown tunic with his red clan plaid slung over his shoulder. He towered over Ailbeart, but the Munro did not back down.

"Do you know this man?" he asked her.

She gave a slight nod, her gaze lifting to lock on Ruari's brown eyes. Even though they were the same color as Ailbeart's, they were so much warmer, gold flecks shining in them. She took a small, unconscious step toward him.

"What do you want?" Ailbeart demanded.

"I couldn't help but overhear your declaration. My lady, have you accepted his proposal?" he asked, the warmth in his gaze disappearing in an instant.

"Nay, I…" she looked from one man to the other. Ailbeart's fingers dug into her skin, silencing her. She nearly screamed at the painful assault, but she'd always been taught not to make a scene in public. She held her tongue, but the look on Ailbeart's face filled her with terror.

"She has no say in the matter. The lady will be my wife in a sennight, and you are to leave us. Now!" His voice came out in a raw bellow and a crowd gathered around them.

Juliana wished to run and hide, but the man had an iron-grip on her arm.

"Let go," Ruari said, grabbing Ailbeart's other arm. "You're hurting her."

"I'll touch her as I please since she is my betrothed. 'Tis no concern of yours."

Ruari lowered his face until it nearly touched Ailbeart's. "Let. Go. Of. Her."

Ailbeart pinched harder, sending searing waves of pain down her arm.

A growl came from deep inside Ruari and he grabbed Ailbeart by the throat, lifting him in the air, which forced him to finally drop his punishing grip from Juliana's arm.

He tossed Ailbeart to the side as if he were naught but a bale of hay and, the man landed on his arse. His face lit up with a fury unlike anything she'd ever seen.

Juliana turned and ran.

"I'll have you whipped for touching me," Ailbeart shouted, but Ruari didn't mind him. He followed her instead.

"Juliana, are you hale? Please allow me to escort you back to the abbey. I'll get you safely away from that brute." She stopped running for a moment, noticing the three Munro guards closing in around her, their swords drawn as if to protect her from Ruari...but Ruari was defending her. It was Ailbeart who'd harmed her.

Five Cameron guards came up behind Ruari, drawing their weapons as well.

The Munro chieftain came up behind the group, brushing the dirt from his clothing. He spoke to his guards first. "Stand down unless he touches me again." He moved in front of Ruari. "This marriage will take place, regardless of anything you say. She is mine and you'd better learn it now."

Ten more Munro guards appeared, and their laird gripped Juliana's elbow, although less cruelly this time, and led her away from the group. She glanced over her shoulder back at Ruari and said, "I'm sorry."

"Say the word, Juliana, and I'll kill him."

But she said nothing, instead walking off with the man who'd hurt her.

Oh, how she wished she were in Ruari's arms instead. But if she allowed Ruari to take her away, people would be hurt, and it would all be her fault. She'd seen enough men die.

———◆———

Ruari couldn't stop the pounding of his heart as he watched Juliana being pushed by the bastard Munro. It had seemed like fate when he'd first seen her at the stalls. She'd been on his mind, although this outing had been his attempt at a diversion. The whole family had come along, even Neil, and he hadn't found it in himself to deny Brin's joyful invitation.

Then he'd seen her walking arm in arm with that old man. As if that hadn't been bad enough, Munro was clearly not a man who'd treat her well. He'd squeezed her hard enough to leave bruises on her soft flesh, an image that would haunt his dreams.

He'd offered to help, but she'd said nothing.

What was he to do when she didn't seem to want his help? He couldn't possibly let her marry such a brute, could he?

He stopped and looked at Padraig, a sheepish look on his face. Padraig said, "Just say the word and I'll go with you. Challenge the bastard. I saw the way he touched and spoke to her. He's no man."

He stared after her, wishing more than anything that she'd chosen him, but she hadn't. "She doesn't seem to want anything to do with me."

The crowd dissipated, and Neil came up from behind him. "When are you going to grow a pair of bollocks, Cameron? You should have taken him down."

"Kill a laird here in front of a crowd? They'd have my head on a pike in the middle of the festival before the sun drops." Why did Neil always know exactly how to goad him? The man seemed determined to make his life miserable.

He was damn sick of him.

Aedan and Jennie came up behind him with Tara, Riley, and Brin. "Nay, Neil. He did the right thing. This was not the place for a major battle. There are bairns here with their parents. Festivals are for everyone, not for swordfights." He clasped his brother's shoulder in encouragement.

"You're much bigger than him, Uncle Ruari," Brin said

knowingly. "You could have beaten him easily."

"But he didn't wish to start a fight," Aedan said. "'Tis the wrong place. Learn from that. True, the man was not treating her properly, and we were all witness to it. Ruari, I wouldn't blame you for challenging him, but please wait until we are away from here. If you wish to fight for her hand, then you should approach him back at the abbey."

"Why allow them to leave and have him think he's won?" Neil asked.

Aedan said, "Because if you didn't notice, a lass under twenty summers stood in the middle and would have surely been hurt. And I have my wife and two daughters with me."

"I wouldn't have wished to see a brawl in the middle of a festival," Jennie added. "Neil, I have to question your motives. Are you trying to taunt Ruari into fighting?"

"Thank you, dear sister, but I can handle myself." He appreciated the sentiment, he didn't want to feel like he was hiding behind his sister-in-law's skirts. "Neil is showing poor judgment again, something he's done more often of late." He cast him a sideways glare but said nothing because his nieces and nephew were present. "I'll not forget how the man treated the lady. You can count on that."

Tara asked, "Who would want to witness a brawl here? You did the right thing, Uncle Ruari. The man was a brute."

Padraig grinned, his white teeth shining. "I would have. And I would have gladly assisted him."

"Me, too," Brin said.

Ruari shook off his anger to the best of his ability, then said, "I need to think. I'll head back to Cameron land."

"As you wish," Aedan said, "Find something for Mama and bring it home for her, will you not? She could use one of those warmers for her hands. She's worn the others thin."

"We'll find it for her, Ruari," Jennie said. "Go if you

like."

Riley asked, "Why not go to the log toss first, Uncle Ruari? You might feel better afterward."

Ruari couldn't help but be surprised at the insight of his young niece. He always felt better after exertion, and the log toss was just what he needed to exorcise his temper. The blood running through his veins felt particularly hot just now. But if he tossed some logs and perchance pretended he was tossing a certain laird instead... "Good idea. 'Tis where I'll go first, then I'm heading home."

What an odd but accurate thought to have come from his niece.

<hr/>

Juliana had been tossed up onto her horse's back so quickly that she'd needed to scramble for Winnie's mane to keep from going over the other side. She settled and stared at her escort.

The face she'd thought so affable at first was twisted with rage. Ailbeart Munro was still furious with Ruari Cameron.

Or was he furious with her? She wasn't sure.

Oh, how she wished she'd run with Ruari.

She waited for the guards to mount while Ailbeart gave them his instructions. Her gaze traveled the area, halting on the log toss. She'd seen the competition before, but she hadn't been the least bit interested in the past. That changed in a moment.

Ruari strode over to a massive log, his back to her, and stripped his tunic off, tossing it aside. His bronzed skin shone like a beacon, calling for her attention, and she gave it to him. He bent over the log, lifting it with a roar, the muscles in his back rippling with his every movement. Her gaze locked on his now-glistening skin as he used all his strength to send the log off into the distance.

The crowd roared as the log flew well beyond that of any

of the other contenders, his friends clapping his shoulders, congratulating him on his spectacular toss. He proceeded to toss another one and the crowd roared even louder.

All she could do was stare at the fine specimen of a man standing not far from her. She wanted to run her hands down his back, feel the hardness of his muscles, and taste the salt in his sweat. Her mouth went dry as he turned to face her. He didn't notice her at first, and she took in his flat abdomen and his bulging chest muscles, a smattering of brown hair begging for her touch. She'd wondered what color it would be.

He laughed when they called his name as the winner, and he chugged on a skin, pouring some of the water over his head.

The water cascaded down his powerful, sinewy muscles, the drops glistening in the sun that had just popped through the clouds, and she had the sudden urge to lick every one of those drops from his body as he swung his wet locks back and forth.

But then his gaze found hers and he froze.

In that moment, heat carried across the field, drenching her body in a sweat that seemed to come from him. She swallowed as his gaze bore through her, as if she sat her horse naked, the fur of the horse tickling her in places she'd never felt before, making her want to rub herself against the beast.

But the moment ended when the judge grabbed Ruari's hand and held it up over his head to declare him the winner, pulling his gaze from hers and turning him toward the cheering crowd.

At that same exact moment, Ailbeart yanked her by her hair, his horse now next to hers, and said, "Do not ever embarrass me like that again." Chapter Sixteen

When they arrived back at the abbey, Juliana dismounted on her own just as Ailbeart made his way over to her. His demeanor had changed back to the way it had been prior to their run-in with Ruari, so she thanked him for his gifts and tried to make her way past him, but he stopped her.

"Lady Juliana, forgive me for my actions. I lost my temper when that man came near you. I fear I will never like another man looking at the woman who is mine. Could we have a brief repast so we can talk?"

"Nay, I need to lie down. It was a most exhausting day, though I do thank you for it and for my gifts." It was almost time for the evening meal, but she had no desire to be around such a cruel man. She just wished to go to bed and speak with Joan.

She held her breath, but he finally agreed, taking her arm to help her inside. "Aye, festivals can be quite exhausting for gentle ladies."

As soon as he released her, she dashed off to the room she shared with her sister. Once inside, she collapsed on the bed, tossing her gifts off to the side. She never wished to look at them again. Joan came in moments later and said, "I heard it did not go well."

She nearly burst into tears, but instead stood up and said, "Please help me into my night rail. I don't wish to step outside this chamber until the morrow."

Joan hurried to assist her, helping her release her gown's laces. But as soon as her sister tugged off one of the sleeves, she gasped and said, "Who did this to you?"

"What?" She turned her arm over, just then noticing the huge bruises on the tender underside of her arm. "Oh my."

"Juliana, that must be verra sore. I'm going for a poultice right away."

"Please help me get undressed first. I wish to lie down. 'Twas a verra trying day, and I'll be happy to tell you about it, but first I must get comfortable and find something to eat." She must have looked like she was ready to collapse because her sister stopped fussing at once.

"Oh, dear. Of course I'll help you. We have all the time

in the world to talk. After I help you into your night rail, I'll find you something to eat, just a light repast."

Once her sister left, she settled onto the bed, propped up on the plump pillows, reviewing all that happened and wondering how much to tell her sister. After much thought, she decided to tell her everything because she desperately needed advice.

But she fell asleep instead and dreamed about a handsome man tossing a log.

———◆———

Juliana slept until the morning, to her surprise. Her sister shook her awake. "Juliana, Papa wishes to see you in the hall. You must get up. I'll help you get dressed. You can tell me everything later, but I'll give you a hint. He wants to take you back to marry Ailbeart by the end of the week. You cannot. You must put him off. I'll tell him you have your courses."

Very little registered with Juliana. Her brain, still foggy from sleep, barely functioned enough for her to recall what had happened the day before.

It seemed stuck on the image of a handsome Scot tossing a log into the air.

She forced herself to a sitting position and mumbled, "What? They wish me to leave? And I think 'twill not be a lie to tell Papa I have my courses."

"Good. 'Tis what we'll say. No respectable lady travels at that time of the moon." Joan tugged the covers back and pulled on her arm. "You must still arise. They'll demand to see you."

"Ow," she howled, clutching her upper arm where Ailbeart had gripped her so hard.

Joan's brow furrowed as peered at the back of her sore arm. "That bastard. 'Twas him, was it not?"

"Joan, why do you hate him so? You hated him before he hurt me. Can you tell me why?

"I'll explain when we have more time, but you must get dressed. Mayhap we can tell them you've decided to stay and take your vows after all." Her sister bustled around the chamber, arranging her clothes, finding her a linen square so that she might wash her face.

Juliana took the linen square and a sliver of soap over to the basin and started her ablutions. "But I don't wish to become a nun," she said, rinsing her face. After the sinful thoughts she'd had about Ruari Cameron with his tunic removed, she'd best spend her time in the chapel confessing.

"That doesn't matter. We just need them to go away."

A sharp knock at the door stopped their conversation. Sister Grace said, "Your sire asked me to report to you that if you are not both below stairs in a quarter hour, he'll be coming up for you." Then she giggled. "Though you need not worry. Mother Matilda would never allow a man up here in the women's quarters. But do hurry."

Her light lilt made the threat sound almost pleasant, which was surely not as he'd intended.

"We'll be right there, Sister Grace."

In a matter of moments, they descended the staircase into the hall. Juliana was pleased to see many people hurrying about—at least she would not have to face the man who'd abused her alone. Food had been set out on the side table and many of the novices and nuns were still eating. Ailbeart headed directly toward them as soon as her feet hit the floor.

He clasped her hands in his and asked, "May I have a moment of your time, Lady Juliana? Before you sit down, if you please."

Joan had already made her way to their sire, whispering in his ear, so Juliana agreed. They moved into a small alcove, still within sight of the rest of the chamber, and he gushed over her.

"My lady, my apologies for my actions yesterday. I should

not have lost my temper with the Cameron's brother. The abbess has told me he is an honorable man and was probably only concerned for your safety. I vow 'twill not happen again. I'd also like to give you this as a pledge of my troth to you." He slipped a ring onto her finger—a golden band featuring a large green stone. "Will you forgive me?"

Joan walked up behind him, her face twisted into a scowl. "You should apologize for hurting her arm, you beast," she seethed.

Juliana removed the ring and handed it back to the laird. He took it, casting her a strange look, but said nothing. She was shocked by the way her sister continued to speak to the laird of Clan Munro. Would his temper flare as quickly as it had yesterday? Part of her feared for her sister, but surely he wouldn't dare touch her in such a public place.

"Sister Joan," he said at last, "I don't know of what you speak, but please allow us a few moments of privacy."

Joan took her hand and carefully pushed the sleeve of her gown up, revealing the multi-colored large bruises on her upper arm. Juliana couldn't help but wince as her sister turned her arm to show him.

"Where did you get that?" Ailbeart said, his demeanor so sincere it baffled her. Was he that good at hiding the truth? "I'll kill any man who harms even a hair on your head. If anyone dares to touch your flesh again, I'll have them flayed alive, at the end of my own whip."

"I believe it happened when you gripped me tight after Lord Cameron appeared," she whispered, a wee bit afraid of his reaction.

"You lie," he said, a fury crossing his face before he covered it. "My apologies. I don't recall handling you roughly at all. Mayhap it happened when you were on horseback. No matter. 'Tis in the past and I wish to speak only of the future. I'd like to escort you back to Munro land, along with your sire, so we can plan the nuptials to commence in five days."

Her sire came up behind him, clearing his throat as if he were uncomfortable. "Excuse me, Laird Munro, but something has come to my attention and I have decided to allow Juliana to stay at the abbey for three or four more days. We shall return to escort her at a later time." Her father appeared gravely embarrassed. "If I could have a moment of your time, Laird?"

Ailbeart glanced at the three faces, Joan's chin lifting a notch, then turned to Juliana and said, "Excuse us for a moment, my dear."

The two men stepped far enough away that they could not be overheard.

After her father spoke, things changed. Ailbeart crossed his arms and said loud enough for all to hear, "I do not care. That changes nothing."

Her sire said, "But I do care. She is at a tender age, and she will remain here for at least three more days."

Juliana, shocked her sire would stand up to the man for her sake, could not have been more pleased.

The laird was not happy, but he must have accepted her sire's decision because he made his way back to her and gave a slight bow. "I shall return for you in three days. I hope you will be feeling better by then."

He spun on his heel and left.

Juliana breathed a deep sigh of relief.

A lot could happen in three days.

———◆———

Ruari was out in the lists when he noticed several horses leaving the abbey in a cloud of dust. The distance was too great for him to make out any details. He dropped his sword and said to Padraig, "I must see who is leaving. I pray 'tis not Juliana."

"Would you chase after her? Or mayhap you'd get down on bended knee and beg for her hand? Or would you go straight for Munro and take him down? 'Tis what I'd do if I were you." The excited glint in Padraig's eyes told Ruari how much he loved the excitement of the situation. "Mayhap sing a song declaring your love for her. I'm sure she'd accept your hand if only to get you to stop."

He couldn't help but smile, even as his heart hammered in his chest. Setting off for the stables at a fast pace, he said, "You'd love for me to go blaze a trail toward them and knock that brute off his horse, would you not?"

Padraig scampered after him. "Aye, would you, if I were to beg? I'll be right behind you. I'll take down three of his guards so you can focus on the hedgehog."

"Nay, Aedan would have me whipped for something like that."

"Why are you so afraid of your brother?" he asked, as he finally caught up.

"I'm not afraid of him."

"Then you're afraid he'll have a reason not to make you his second."

There was no denying it was true. Plenty of other men had what it took to fill that position, and he hated the thought of being passed over again. But something else had also been niggling at him. Why did his mother keep reminding him that Aedan was the stronger brother? She didn't always use that word, of course, but she'd told him Aedan was older, more prepared, and had better judgment. He'd listened to her ruminations on the state of their brotherhood for years. Of late, she'd said it much more often, but he had no idea why.

Shaking the thought off, he retrieved his horse and mounted, then started to ride toward the abbey, Padraig hurrying to keep up with him.

"Stop thinking about your mother," his friend said. "She's stuck on when the two of you were bairns. It happens as someone gets older."

He reined in his horse, turning to face Padraig. "How the hell would you know what I'm thinking?" He was horrified that Padraig had guessed the direction of his thoughts. Was it so obvious?

"Because I see how upset you are whenever you leave her, and I've noticed how you avoid visiting her. I understand, Ruari. My mother always used to compare me to Roddy, praising him for being more serious than I am. More driven. But now that I'm here, she's starting to see me differently."

"Truly?"

"Aye, but my sire always told her to stop comparing us. We're not the same, and neither are you and Aedan, and that's a good thing. You need to make a bold move. I'm telling you to do something Aedan doesn't expect from you. 'Tis the only way you'll feel like your own man."

Perhaps Padraig had a point.

First, he had to see what was taking place at the abbey. Then he'd have a better idea about what kind of bold move he could make.

Perhaps he'd steal a lass right out of the abbey.

CHAPTER SEVENTEEN

ONCE HER SIRE HAD LEFT with the Munro and all his guards, Juliana lowered herself into a chair in front of the hearth. "I'm cold, Joan." Tired, cold, frustrated, and confused.

The hall was nearly empty, just a couple of serving maids cleaning up and taking things to the kitchens. "Joan, can you give me another reading lesson, please? They may make me leave soon. Do you think I can learn in three days?" She stared into the fire, wondering how her life could have changed so rapidly in such a short time.

Her sister chuckled, moving over to the basket next to the hearth and pulling out a thick fur to place over Juliana's lap. "Nay, I cannot teach you in three days. But I can get you started. We had a good beginning the other day, learning your letters. That must come first. Let me see how much you remember from your previous lesson."

A tear slipped out of the side of Juliana's eye as she stared into the flames.

Joan pulled a chair up beside hers. "Tell me what you're thinking," she said, patting Juliana's hand. "We didn't have much time to talk last eve."

She turned to face her sister, fighting the torrent of tears that threatened to drench her cheeks. "Can you please tell me why you hate Ailbeart Munro?"

Her sister let out a deep sigh. "I met him when we were

younger. But it doesn't matter what I think. What's your impression of him?"

Juliana stared into the flames. "One minute he was so nice, and the next he became nasty and cruel. He was so apologetic this morn that I almost believed him."

"What did he apologize for? He denied hurting you."

"He lost his temper when Ruari appeared." Her hand moved up to the back of her head, massaging the spot where he'd yanked on her hair, causing a headache that still hadn't relented.

"'Twould be dangerous to marry a man with such a violent temper," Joan said softly.

"I must say I agree with you. His temper frightens me. He attempted to give me a ring as a symbol of our betrothal, but I gave it back to him. If not for Papa, I know not what he would have said." She stared at the flames, remembering how beautiful the ring had looked on her finger. "He bought me beautiful ribbons and slippers. I've not had such nice things before. You know how worn my slippers are."

"Oh, Juliana." She touched her hand. "Those are just things. They don't really matter. 'Tis what is in your heart that matters, and I think his heart is black. Did you agree to marry him?"

"Nay, he doesn't seem to think I have a choice. He said as much yesterday." Her face fell and the tears finally slid down her cheek. "Papa is set on me marrying him."

"But your heart is not in a marriage to Ailbeart, is it?"

She shook her head, swiping at her tears. "Nay, I do not wish to marry such a cruel man."

"You'd rather become a nun, am I not correct?"

She shrugged, turning her head away so she wouldn't see the disappointment in her sister's gaze.

"Is this about Ruari Cameron?" her sister asked, hesitantly.

She nodded and said, "I think I love him." Then she burst into tears, sobbing so hard her shoulders bobbed up and down.

"Are you sure? Do you know him well enough to love him?"

She nodded furiously, then said, "You wouldn't understand, but he's the only one I want. I know it from the way I felt when we kissed. I love Ruari Cameron."

Joan just stared at her, but she didn't look angry or judgmental. She didn't insist that Juliana stay and become a nun.

"What am I to do?" she bawled.

"Don't worry," her sister said. "I'll take care of everything."

She was so busy sobbing that she didn't stop to wonder what Joan meant by that.

———◆———

It was the middle of the night and Ruari was still awake, pacing in the great hall. He'd learned Juliana's sire and Laird Munro had gone back to Munro land and would return to the abbey in three days. He'd spent several sleepless hours pacing, but he still couldn't decide what to do about the situation.

He *wanted* to marry Juliana. The idea of her marrying the bastard who'd hurt her made him want to bellow from the tallest mountains in the Highlands. Nay, that beautiful lass with brown eyes and soft pink lips deserved to be treated gently, with honor and love.

Padraig came in from outside and clucked his tongue. "Still can't get her off your mind, you lovesick laddie?"

"Must you always wear that wise-arse grin? Why aren't you abed, anyway?"

Padraig sat down in a chair and settled his boots on a bench in front of him. "Aye, I must. Does it bother you? Because if it does, you've a simple way to get rid of it. Do something bold. If you like the girl a *wee* bit, don't bother. If you like her way more than that, then you better act before Munro returns, and to hell with Aedan and your mother. They'll deal with whatever you do. Can you live with her marrying Munro?"

The lad had a point.

"You're still thinking on it. My brother left home, married his lass, and is happier than a hedgehog with a giant pile of caterpillars in front of it. My sire and mother rarely see him, so when they do, they gush over him like he's the long-lost bairn. Yet he's too busy to notice because he can't take his gaze off his wife. Don't you wish to be that happy?"

"Would you stop making such good points? You've convinced me. I'm leaving."

"Now?" he asked, dropping his booted feet to the ground. "I didn't mean now. Where the hell are you going?"

"I'm going to find Juliana Clavelle," he said with a wink as he strode out the door with a grin. "And aye, this is *my* wise-arse grin."

He couldn't help but hum now that he'd made his decision, although he still needed to figure out a way to see her. He saddled his horse and rode to the abbey, stopping at the stables to ask if there'd been any visitors today.

The stable lad was sound asleep, and he only lifted his head long enough to shake it before falling back into a deep slumber. Ruari left his horse inside and made his way around to the back door of the abbey, where the kitchens were located. Two guards were stationed outside the door, but he knew both of them and said, "I just need to grab something to eat."

They both yawned and waved him in. Although the abbey had been attacked before, it was rare, and it went without saying that no Cameron would ever do such a thing. Most Highlanders had an inherent respect for anyone wearing the cloth.

He peeked inside the door to the great hall, and to his surprise, Juliana stood in front of the hearth, staring at the now-retreating flames within it. She held her hands over the heat, bending over to warm her fingers.

He didn't wish to scare her, but his gut urged him to race to her side. A wild part of him wanted to grab her around the waist and spin her through the air. This lass did something to him, and the desire to hold her built with each step he took across the cold stone floor.

The sound of his boots echoed in the empty hall, and she spun around to stare at him. "Ruari? 'Tis really you?"

"Aye," he whispered, "please don't send me away. I wish to speak with you."

She didn't send him anywhere, instead opening her arms to him. He ran the rest of the way to her, and she wrapped her arms around his neck.

"You're shivering," he whispered into her neck as he embraced her, reveling in her sweet scent of wildflowers.

"I know, I am so cold, but I probably shouldn't be here with you. I'm just in my night rail," she said, taking a step back to stare up at him. "Why are you here?"

"I just had to see you. After seeing you with Munro…I just…" He scratched his head, wondering how to continue from here, yet wishing to make sure he chose the right words. There was so much at stake. "May we talk just for a wee bit before you return to your chamber?"

Her gaze locked onto his and she nodded.

He pointed to a chair not far from the hearth. "Sit in this large chair with me. I'll wrap you up and vow to keep you warm." He settled her next to him and held her close, his chin nearly on the top of her head, but he pulled back enough to peek at her. "Are you warm enough?"

"Aye." She didn't say anything else, so he continued.

"I don't know what happened between Stonecroft Abbey and here. We kissed, and mayhap I shouldn't have taken advantage of your innocence in such a way, but I don't regret it. I like you verra much, and my feelings have continued to grow stronger. I offered for your hand, and I thought you said aye, but everything changed after you spoke with your sister. You wouldn't even speak with me on the way back to Lochluin. I thought it was because of your sister, but I wonder if it had something to do with Ailbeart Munro. What happened between us?"

She leaned back to answer him, and the quivering of her pink lips nearly caused him to lose all control. Nay, he'd not taste her again until he found out the truth of her heart.

She dipped her head, then lifted her chin. "Answer me honestly. Would you have offered for me if the abbess hadn't told you to do so?"

"Is that what you think?" he asked in shock. "That I only want you because the abbess said so?"

"Or forced you. Is it true?"

"Nay, nay. I would have offered for you without her suggestion. While I would have liked to properly court you, we don't have that option. I'm ready to marry you now. Munro doesn't deserve you, nor will he treat you with respect. I saw him mishandle you already."

Her gaze softened and she reached up to touch the stubble on his jaw, tracing her finger across his chin to the other side of his face. "I don't wish to marry Ailbeart Munro, I wish to marry you. I wish we could take our time, too, but it cannot be. My sire intends to force me to marry the Munro, and I know not what to do."

Her hand fell from his face and her gaze dropped, but he tilted her chin up to him. His lips met hers in a searing kiss that quickly turned tender. He wanted to show her how much he respected and admired her. How much he wished for them to have a future together.

He ended the kiss and said, "I asked your sire for your hand, but he refused me, saying you are to marry Munro."

"Then what are we to do?" she asked, the worry and fear in her voice evident.

"They're to return in three days? We could marry on our own before that, if you'll have me. Will your sister support you?"

"I'm not sure, but she no longer seems opposed to a match between us. I know she doesn't like Munro."

He stood up and tugged her close, enjoying the feel of her in his arms, her soft curves molding to his body. He could hold her like this forever.

Forever didn't last long enough.

She whispered, "I love you, Ruari."

His knees nearly buckled at this declaration. He realized with startling clarity that he no longer needed to wonder what it felt like to love a woman—he knew it. Without question. He kissed her lightly on her lips and said, "Juliana, I think we were meant to be together. 'Tis in the stars, just as my brother always told me would happen someday."

"Do you love me?" The hope in her gaze made him want to sweep her into his arms and run away.

"I do. We belong together and I'll do everything I can to see that it happens. I pledge that to you." A noise caught his ears from behind them.

Her sister came down the staircase and said, "What are you doing, Juliana?" She hadn't shouted and her tone didn't sound angry, but he knew he had to release Juliana.

His love spun around to face her sister, blushing to the tips of the toes he could see sticking out from beneath her night rail.

"We were just talking, Joan. Please don't be upset, but we would like to marry. I don't wish to marry Ailbeart Munro. Will you help us?"

"I'll talk to Papa. But don't worry. If he doesn't agree, I have another idea."

Ruari had no idea what that meant, but he knew her sister to be a strong-minded person. Having her on their side gave him a wee bit of hope.

Which was more than he'd had when he entered the abbey.

CHAPTER EIGHTEEN

———◆———

THE NEXT MORNING, RUARI FELT much more confident. He knew without a doubt that he wanted Juliana for his wife. And it was more than her sweet pouty lips.

Every time he was around her, his heart soared. He loved talking to her, sharing his thoughts with her, and listening to her thoughts in turn.

He'd wondered his whole life what it would be like to truly love a woman. Now he knew.

He headed down to the great hall, humming under his breath, and immediately ran into Padraig. That wise-arse grin was still on his face.

The lad let out a low whistle. "Something's put a wee bounce in your walk, Cameron. Could it be a lass with light brown hair?"

Ruari just arched an eyebrow at his friend. He didn't say his true thoughts, that Juliana's hair was the color of warm sand, not just brown. Or that her lips were the kind that begged to be kissed, and he wished to do much more of that.

Or how it felt to hold her in his arms.

Soothing yet exciting at the same time. Was that possible? He'd never experienced its equal. Had her sister not interrupted them, he likely wouldn't have left.

"What's causing that smile?" Padraig prodded.

Ruari chuckled and said, "I'm off to visit my brother. I'll tell you all later. Meet me in the lists in an hour or so."

Padraig clasped his shoulder and took his leave.

Aedan usually broke his fast with Jennie and their children, but there was no sign of any of them, which meant they'd likely come and gone. Sure enough, he found Aedan seated in his solar, staring off into space as he'd often done as a child.

"You cannot be staring at the stars. 'Tis too bright a day."

His brother jerked his head around and laughed. "Certainly not looking at the stars. I was just thinking."

"Care to share?"

"Nay." His brother offered nothing more. "Are you in need of something?"

"Aye, I'd like your help."

"You have it. What is it?"

"As you know, I wish to marry Juliana Clavelle…"

His brother held his hand up to stop him. "Ruari, she was with Munro at the festival, was she not?"

"Aye."

"And you believe her father will send him away and accept your suit?" Aedan drummed his fingers on the tabletop awaiting his answer.

How did he phrase this correctly? He wanted his brother to listen to him. "He rejected me in favor of Munro. The laird just left and is to return in three to four days to escort her to his land for their marriage, but Juliana is not interested in marrying him and wishes to marry me."

"Ruari, you'll go nowhere if the betrothal has already been made. You're talking about a neighboring laird, albeit a wee distance, it does not change his ranking. You know the way of it. The lass's wishes are usually ignored. I don't know how you can make this work."

Ruari's temper flared. "You won't help your only brother? Should I bring the lass to you so you can see the bruises he inflicted on her arm just because I approached them? Should I remind you that he was married before and is known for being a bastard?"

Aedan got up from his desk and moved around to stand in front of Ruari. "I noticed how he treated her, and you're not wrong about it being a bad match. Are you sure she's not interested in marrying Munro?"

"She is not interested in him. She loves me." His fists clenched at his sides and he didn't care if his brother noticed. If he couldn't count on him, who could he count on?

"And you love her?"

"Aye. Will that not sway you?"

"If you're sure about it. But give me some time to think of a solution. I cannot risk Munro showing up with his guards. I vowed to protect Lochluin Abbey and all that are in it." He sighed and clasped his brother's shoulder. "I'd be pleased to see you happily married, Ruari, but we must do this carefully. I'll speak with her sire when they return."

That wasn't exactly what he'd hoped to hear. He wished to marry her *now*—before Munro returned.

"Thank you, Aedan, but I cannot risk it. I cannot lose her."

———

Juliana couldn't sleep after she'd seen Ruari, simply because her heart was bursting with happiness. She was in love.

And he loved her, too.

She didn't fall asleep until nearly dawn, so she slept most of the next day away.

When she finally climbed out of bed in the middle of the afternoon, her sister was humming a song their mother used to sing to them when they were wee bairns.

Her sister smiled, a big bright smile that made her gasp. She hadn't seen Joan like this in…well, in years. "Good afternoon to you, dear sister."

"Joan, is everything all right? You look happy. Did something happen while I was sleeping?"

"Nay, naught has changed. I was working on something to help teach you your letters." She held up a book, a journal of sorts, in which several pages had already been marked. Her sister flipped through it to show her. "See how much I've done for you already? I thought if I put everything in one place, it would be easier. Once you've eaten, we can continue your lessons."

While she loved this side of her sister, and she so looked forward to learning how to read, something felt off.

Her sister disappeared and returned with a tray of food—a bowl of pottage with a hunk of freshly-baked dark bread. "This was made fresh this morn. It's quite delicious. I helped with the vegetables."

Juliana ate simply because she was famished. But once she was halfway finished, she stopped and asked, "Joan, have you thought of a way to help me deny Laird Munro?"

Her sister gave her an enigmatic smile and said, "Aye." She stared off into space as if enjoying the thought of whatever it was she'd decided to do.

"How?" She took another bite of the bread, chewing slowly as she studied her sister. Why was she acting so strangely? After all these days of wishing for her to be a nun, what had changed her mind?

"Don't you worry about that. I'll talk to Papa. He'll see how right I am."

"Joan, you've encouraged me to take my vows for years, but lately you've been acting like you'd support my wish to marry Ruari."

Her sister sat down on the bed and folded her hands in her lap. "I haven't given up completely in my quest to convince you to take your vows, but I'm beginning to believe mayhap Ruari is right for you. He is a fine man, and you would be a wonderful mother. You must trust that sometimes things happen in unexpected ways. Do not worry yourself. Focus on your letters for now." She stood and started to fuss with various things around the chamber, setting them to rights.

"But Joan, I love him."

Her sister spun around and gave her the oddest look, one she couldn't read, but then she surprised her by saying, "I know you do."

She kissed her forehead and strode out the door. "When I return, I'll start teaching you your letters."

What had happened to her sister?

———◆———

Ruari rushed out of the keep, bolting past several people who attempted to speak with him—the smithy, the armorer, even a stable lad—but he just couldn't take the time to acknowledge anyone. Marching inside the stable, he saddled his horse and led him out the door, refusing to speak with anyone. He'd finally come up with the bold move Padraig had been convincing him to take.

Time was of the essence. He had to persuade Munro to stay away. If he could convince the man that Juliana was not right for him, then Aedan would support him completely.

He hated to be upset with his brother. The Camerons did have an unspoken bond with the abbey. They were the closest clan, so it was their duty to make sure that nothing would upset their presence or their coffers.

Their coffers were mighty deep, so the protection of their wealth was a huge responsibility.

He had his sword and two daggers with him, which he was quite certain he would need now that he'd made his *bold* decision. Ailbeart Munro had a black heart, and he would prove it to all. He'd uncover something about the man to use against him, to force him to stay away from his betrothed. He considered her his soon-to-be wife, and it was his responsibility to protect her.

He was headed toward Munro land to convince the

brute to stay away from Juliana Clavelle.
And nothing would stop him.

CHAPTER NINETEEN

———————

IT WAS NEARLY DARK WHEN he found himself on Munro land. Ruari stopped out of view of the guards, tying his horse to a tree near a burn. It was time to sneak inside the castle and uncover something useful about Ailbeart Munro. There was something about the laird he didn't trust.

Something evil.

"Hold." One guard stopped, holding his hand up to another as if he sensed Ruari's presence. He froze, hiding behind two trees as the guards scanned the area. "I thought I heard something. Did you?"

The other guard listened for a few moments and said, "Nay. Are you certain?"

Neither said anything, listening, but then the first said, "I guess 'twas naught."

"Must have been a wild boar."

They continued on with their duty while Ruari made his way around to the back of the curtain wall, searching for a good place to scale it. When he found a spot where the wall crumbled in enough places to give him footholds, he made his way to the top of the wall. There he paused, praying the dark, moonless night hid his form. He had to be sure of what he would be dropping into.

Seeing nothing beneath him, he dropped soundlessly to the ground. Once there, he paused again, listening for any sounds behind the castle.

All was quiet.

He crept across the grounds, moving between the grasses to silence his footfalls. He had almost reached the back entrance to the keep when he froze.

He could hear a sword being drawn.

And another and another.

Hellfire, he was caught.

He spun around, unsheathing his weapon, and sliced the first of his attackers across his shoulder. The man bellowed and dropped his weapon.

But then he was besieged by a dozen guards, who knocked his weapon out of his hand and beat him to the ground.

"Who is he?" asked one.

"Cameron. Go see if the laird wants to see him or if we can kill him now."

Two guards disappeared, only for one of them to rush back out moments later. "Don't hurt him. Bring him inside to Munro. He wishes to see him."

Ruari cursed himself. Fighting a dozen men would get him nowhere, so he gave up and agreed to walk on his own, following two men who took the lead. They used the back entrance to enter the castle, then shoved him down a passageway and up the three final steps leading into the great hall.

As soon as he was escorted inside, Munro bellowed out to him, "Has something happened to my betrothed, Cameron? 'Tis the only reason you should be on my land. Sneaking about tells me you had other intentions."

"Juliana Clavelle is hale," he said, moving over to stand in front of the bastard seated at his dais with several guards. "I'd like to speak with you in private, Munro."

The man arched a brow while a few of the guards openly laughed at him. "You're an intruder. I have the right to kill you and put your head on a pike in front of my castle. You don't make the rules. You'll say whatever you came to say in front of my men."

Ruari had a bad feeling as the door to the keep opened and several more guards entered, encircling him from behind. Perhaps he should have brought Padraig and a few guards of his own along on his journey. His plan to spy on the brute had failed him terribly. He'd hardly be learning anything he could use against him in the present situation.

He hesitated, but then decided he'd speak his mind regardless of the danger. "Juliana Clavelle will be marrying me, not you. She has no interest in you, so I'm here to ask you to step away from your pursuit of her. Whatever you want with her, 'tis not honorable. There are many other lasses you could marry."

Munro leaned his chair back and guffawed, something that made Ruari's blood boil. Oh, to stop that laughter. The laird abruptly launched to his feet, then swaggered over to him. Standing in front of him, he said two words with careful inflection. "She's mine."

Ruari took a step closer and said, "She wants nothing to do with you, so stop pursuing her. The lass is too tenderhearted for you. I saw how you treated her at the festival, like she was a dog you wished to beat into submission."

"And she'll be my wife in less than a sennight," the man said with a smirk. "If I feel like beating her into submission, I will. I paid her sire good coin for the right to do as I wish to her body, and you can count on the fact that I will. I'm going to offer you one chance to leave on your own before I have my men take care of you my way."

Ruari locked gazes with the fool, and the man's eyes were every bit as cold and cruel as he had expected. Nay, he would never allow such a man to marry Juliana.

"She'll never marry you. You can count on that. Your false attempts to buy her love haven't worked." Padraig's words called to him. He had to do something bold at this point. He considered his options of walking away or fighting two dozen guards and dismissed both of them. He had only one alternative. "Why not meet me in the courtyard with your weapon of choice and we'll settle this now?" Ruari took two steps back for emphasis. "Or are you too soft for the challenge?"

"You were a fool to come here on your own, Cameron. Did you really believe you could sneak inside without being seen? Did you think to kill me in my bed while I slept?"

The smirk on his face told Ruari he wasn't going to fight him. He'd hoped to ignite the man's competitive side, but perhaps he didn't have one.

"You don't have the guts to fight me, do you?" Ruari asked.

Munro's response was to make his way back to his seat behind the dais. "I have a meal to finish," he said. Then he nodded to his guards and said, "Take him outside and show him who will be marrying Lady Juliana. Mess him up good but don't kill him."

"Why not, Chief? We could entertain ourselves for a long time with a slow kill," one of his guards commented.

"I still need a priest from Lochluin Abbey to marry us. They'll not do that if we kill a Cameron."

Seven men headed straight toward him, and Ruari did his best to take as many of the bastards down as he could with his fists, but he knew he wouldn't get very far. The odds were not in his favor.

"Could you not take him outside before there's bloodshed in my hall?" Munro said in a bored tone. "Remember, I don't want him dead. Beat him and send him back on his horse."

The remaining men grabbed him from behind. They carried him out the door while he kicked and punched as many of them as possible. Once they had him outside the gates, three of the men held him down while the rest beat him.

One punch to the face caught him just right and he blacked out.

His last thought was he'd been a fool for certain this time.

———◆———

When he awakened, every part of his body ached, even parts he hadn't known he possessed. He was face down across his horse and the animal moved across the Highland meadow but stopped at a whistle.

Ruari was in too much pain to even lift his head. A familiar voice called out to him, "Are you alive, you fool?"

That could only be Padraig. Ruari tried to speak, but his voice came out in a moan.

"Could you not have at least taken me along with you?" Padraig asked, his voice coming closer. "I know you are too proud to have told your brother or taken any guards, but I could have helped." He put his hand under Ruari's chin and lifted his head. "Hellfire, they did a fine job beating you, did they not? You'll not be able to see Juliana out of those eyes. Your wedding will be postponed for at least a fortnight."

The lad grabbed his horse's reins, stopping him, and said, "Come. You must sit up on your horse. I know it will pain you, but 'tis the only way I can get you home. I know a healer not far from here. We can stop to see her first. Clean you up so you can see the land in front of you."

"Nay, Jennie…"

"You'll not make it to Jennie. We're stopping. The healer's hut is in the forest not a half hour from here. Now sit up."

Ruari groaned as he did his best to shift himself up to sitting on the saddle.

"How many?"

"Seven? Ten? Don't recall much." He spat a stream of blood and dirt off to the side.

Padraig handed him his skin. "Drink, but not too much."

Ruari did as he was told because his head hurt too much for him to think. Why the hell had he been so incautious?

"Never make decisions in anger. You'll always regret them. Did your sire not teach you that?"

Ruari shook his head.

"Seems you prefer to learn in your own way. Stubborn fool. Can you sit?"

Ruari nodded, finally pulling himself the rest of the way up, and took the reins.

"Good. I'll be right behind you. Just stay straight, don't tip, and don't close your eyes. Do you hear me, cousin?"

Ruari nodded, doing his best to follow instructions, but it was truly difficult. After they began moving, his mind did start functioning enough for him to realize he was grateful his cousin had thought to follow him.

The short distance took forever, but they finally arrived at the healer's hut.

"What's her name?" he choked out.

"Grizella," Padraig said. "She may not have the talent of Jennie, but she's been around a long time. My mother knows all the healers in the land, especially the older ones." He dismounted, then stopped Ruari's fall as he tried to do the same. "You're barely walking. I may not get you home for a sennight." He managed to position him so Ruari leaned against him for support. "And when the hell did you get so large across the shoulders?"

Grizella saw them coming and greeted them at the door of her small hut, situated close to a nearby burn. "Is that not the Cameron lord?" she asked, leaning on a shortened piece of wood with a gnarl at the end that she could grip with her hand. A diminutive person, she seemed even shorter because of her rounded shoulders. Her uneven gait carried her across to the burn to fill an urn with water as she motioned for the two to enter her hut.

"Aye, 'tis Ruari Cameron, Aedan's only brother," Padraig

said with a groan as he squeezed through the small door with Ruari still leaning on him. "A few Munros had some fun with him."

Grizella followed them in, clucking her tongue, and directed Padraig to set him down on a pallet off to the side. The hut was suffused with the smell of a fine stew roasting over the hearth, along with the scent of multiple dried herbs. "Get yourself a bowl of stew for getting this big lad here alive," the older healer said, waving to Padraig.

Padraig settled him on the pallet, then went for the stew, filling a bowl to the brim.

"Are you not Doirin's husband?" the healer asked as she approached the pallet. "The poor lass who died too young?"

"Aye," Padraig said with a mouthful of food of stew. "He was."

"You knew her?" Ruari asked. It surprised him to hear it. With Jennie as their chieftain's wife, no one from Clan Cameron had much call to visit another healer. Besides, Doirin had never mentioned such a thing to him.

"Well, my lord, I feel compelled to tell you something while I clean up those wounds."

Ruari winced when she started with the one deep wound he had from a sword.

"Sorry, my lord, but this one gets cleaned first. 'Tis the most likely to fester. I'll clean it, sew it up, then apply my poultice, the same one your brother's dear wife uses." She reached for another linen square and dipped it into the basin of cool water.

"Do as you must. I'll not move." He gritted his teeth as she did her worst. "What was it you wished to tell me?

She sighed and said, "Sometimes I dinnae like my healing chores. Your wife came to me often to acquire the potion that would keep her from getting with child."

Shock seemed to banish his pain. Ruari sat up to stare at her. "What did you say? I fear my mind is clouded with fever already."

"Nay, my lord." She pushed his shoulders back down onto the pallet and continued to clean the blood and dirt from his skin. "'Struth. She did not wish to carry. Ever."

Padraig came over to stand at the end of his pallet, gawking at them while he continued to slurp his stew. He shook his head as he swallowed. "I may not have spent much time with her, but I'm not surprised to hear it. Your wife wasn't good for you, my friend."

Ruari jolted where he lay. "There is a potion for such a thing? How does it work? Do you lose a bairn once you're carrying or…"

Grizella's gnarled hand settled on his arm. "Lad, you've no need to know the details. She did not wish to become with child and I gave her what she needed."

"But why? Why would you do that?" Ruari was stunned that the possibility existed, much less that it worked. "Why not tell me?"

"Och, you ask good questions, my lord. All I'll say is that I've always considered it my duty as a healer to help the person who walks through that door. 'Tis not my place to pass judgment. I'd never kill a live bairn, but I can easily help prevent one from happening."

Ruari lay back and stared at the thatch over his head. That last day he'd begged Doirin to see Jennie, hoping she could help them, and Doirin had adamantly refused.

She'd feared that he would learn the truth.

And that was why she'd ridden away in such a fury.

Or had it been sheer panic?

Not because of something he'd done. She'd been fearful of the possibility that she would be caught.

As far as he was concerned, Doirin might as well have been unfaithful.

She hadn't cared for him at all.

CHAPTER TWENTY

JULIANA'S SIRE AND AILBEART MUNRO returned three days later, as promised. The sick feeling she'd been harboring inside her gut turned suddenly worse. Each day, she'd hoped Ruari would return and claim her. That he'd take her to wife like he'd promised. But he hadn't come. He hadn't come, and now time had run out.

Joan was always quick to remind her there was another solution—she could still take her vows—but Juliana's heart wasn't in it.

And so, she'd be leaving her sister and going off to marry the chieftain of Clan Munro.

He greeted her immediately in the hall. "You look especially lovely this day. You grow more beautiful every time I see you. How do you fare?" He took her hand and kissed the back of it, leaving a wet mark that made her want to cringe.

It struck her again that the man's looks didn't match his nature. He was particularly dashing today, his hair neatly combed even after traveling across the windy Highland meadows.

"Where is the ring I gave you?" He held up both of her hands to check for it.

The hard edge in his tone made her tremble.

"I gave it back to you," she said, suddenly afraid of what he would do next.

He gave her an odd look, spinning on his heel and going off to speak to one of his men, who promptly nodded, though she had no idea what they discussed.

Returning with a smile on his face, he said to her, "My apologies. I was wrong. My second reminded me that I left it in my keep. No matter. I'll place it on your finger as soon as we arrive at Munro Castle."

She didn't quite know what to say, so she just smiled.

He went on, "My clan is anxious to meet their lady. I'll take you to Edinburgh and hire the finest dressmaker to make a new wardrobe for you. The mistress of my clan must look appropriately regal." His gaze traveled down the length of her simple wool gown, stopping at two places—her breasts and the place it was worn from her hands settling on her lap.

She resisted the urge to cover herself.

They gathered together at a trestle table near the hearth. Joan sat beside her, holding her hand for encouragement, her sire and Ailbeart across the table.

"Papa, I'd like to travel with you, if you don't mind," Joan announced, something that she and Juliana hadn't discussed.

"Why?" His gaze narrowed at Joan.

Joan didn't seem put off by his response. "If you recall, I had asked that Juliana spend a moon with me. You agreed to send her for a fortnight, but our time together has been drastically shortened. I'd like to spend as much time as possible with her. We can still talk if we ride abreast."

"Nay, you need to stay here. You are a nun and should not be riding about. I'll take care of Juliana."

To her surprise, Joan shifted to look at Ailbeart. "Laird Munro, if you please, I would like a word alone with my sire."

He nodded politely, although Juliana couldn't help but think it was a false gesture. "I'd be happy to step aside so that you might say your goodbyes. Clavelle, I'll meet you at the stables within the hour so we can be on our way."

"'Tis not necessary," their sire said, glaring at Joan.

She quickly retorted, "Aye, 'tis most necessary."

Munro stood and held his palm up to their father, staying him. "'Tis no problem. I would expect a private farewell."

As soon as he left the hall, their father exploded, "Joan, you must stop annoying our guest. Juliana will be married to him soon, and I do not wish to anger him. He is a powerful nobleman."

"Papa, I asked him to leave because I wish to speak with you. Can you not see that he is not right for Juliana?"

Richard Clavelle's face turned a dark shade of red. "You will not try to undermine the arrangements I've made for your sister. Out of respect for the church, I allowed her to come here to see if she'd like to follow your path, but it's clear she will be much happier married and caring for bairns. Stop trying to remake her in your own image."

All this time, no one had asked Juliana what she wanted for the future. No one had cared. She decided it was time for her to speak her mind, whether they wished to listen or not. Even if Ruari did not still care for her. "Papa, you are correct about one thing."

His face relaxed, and though she knew he'd not be happy about the rest of her statement, she plunged ahead. "I am not interested in taking my vows, but I don't wish to marry Laird Munro. I love Ruari Cameron. He is the Cameron chieftain's brother, so he is of noble blood, and he is a most honorable man. I wish you would reconsider…"

She stopped because her father abruptly stood from the table, knocking the bench over. "You will both hear me now. Juliana, you will marry Laird Munro in less than a sennight, and that decision is final. I care nothing for this upstart Ruari Cameron. Joan, you will not travel with us. I blame you for putting these foolish ideas into her head. You were always a difficult lass, and now you're trying to poison your sister. You'll marry him, Juliana, and that's final!" His last words were spoken in a roar.

Joan did not back down. "He paid you heavily with coin, did he not?"

"I will not answer that. The decision is made and it is final. I make the decisions for my daughters because I'm your sire and I know best. A lass is not smart enough to make her own decisions."

Joan's face twisted with anger, but she didn't respond. Juliana couldn't think of anything to say either. She'd never seen her sire so angry, so cruel. She didn't know what to do. She didn't know if there was anything she *could* do. The law dictated that her sire could make arrangements for her as he saw fit.

If only Ruari had come for her…

Now, she feared it was too late.

———

Ruari lifted his head off the pillow of his bed, groaning as pain coursed through him. Would it never end?

"How many days have passed since I saw the healer, Padraig?" His friend had just entered the chamber with two goblets of ale and a hunk of bread. He forced himself to sit up and accepted the drink, gulping greedily.

"Three," the lad replied, biting off a chunk of bread. "Hellfire, but your cook makes the best bread ever."

"Three? What the hell! Why didn't you wake me? I have to marry Juliana before her sire returns for her. 'Tis the only way." He threw back the covers and shifted his legs to the side of the bed.

"Because your brother stopped in after his wife checked you over. He said if you tried moving any sooner, he'd tie us both to the bed. I like you, cousin, but not enough to be tied to a bed with you."

Ruari groaned and stood up to grab his plaid from the chest next to the wall, nearly collapsing to the floor. Padraig dropped his loaf of bread and barely managed to catch him. "Cameron, you have not eaten in three days. You'll not be able to stand up until you eat something." Ruari ran his hand down his leg. "I only had a few bruises," he said, panting. "Why is this so difficult?"

"Because they beat the shite out of you. I'd say three fists for each bruise. Not to mention the twenty stitches Grizella placed."

He sat down, gasping at the effort it had taken him to stand. "Is Juliana still at the abbey?"

"Aye. But her sire's returned for her, and I hear they'll be leaving by midday. 'Tis why I'm here—to get you up before she leaves."

"Many thanks for that, but you could have awakened me yesterday." He dressed himself, the work painstakingly slow, and grabbed two daggers from his chest.

"You'll not beat anyone if you don't gain some strength back," Padraig observed as Ruari put his boots on. "You must eat, fool." He'd settled into a chair and retrieved his hunk of bread.

"Then I'll eat on the way there." Although he could not deny Padraig had a point. He was struggling to put on his boots, his body weaving back and forth.

"If you're wise, you'll speak with your brother about sending someone with you this time."

"Are you not coming with me?" he asked, arranging the daggers inside his boots.

"For certes, but Munro has twenty warriors with him. I'm sure many of them who are with him"—he waved at Ruari as if to indicate his poor state—"are the same ones who had their fun with you. Think you the two of us can take on twenty, especially in the condition you're in?"

Ruari moved over to the door and stopped, turning to his friend, still sitting there chewing on his bread. He barked, "Are you quite comfortable, Grant? Am I interrupting your rest? Are you capable of chewing while we walk down the stairs?"

Padraig wrinkled his nose and said, "That depends."

"On what?" Ruari bellowed.

"On whether you are smart enough to ask your brother for help. I'm not going with you if you're going to your death. I'd rather chew on bread than watch you skewered by twenty men. Your face still looks like hell. Your lass won't want to marry you looking as you do."

Ruari growled. "Fine. I'll speak with my brother, take a dozen guards or so, and grab a pheasant's leg on the way out. Is there anything else I need to do to make you happy?"

"Nay. I'm right behind you." He jumped out of his chair with a chuckle and followed Ruari down the stairs. "Do not fault me for your own stubbornness."

A few minutes later, a hunk of cheese in hand, Ruari caught up with his brother in the courtyard. "Aedan, I need at least a dozen men to go after Juliana."

"I'd prefer to send them to beat the men who dared to hurt my brother. I just need you to tell me where to send them." Aedan looked him up and down, probably to decide whether or not Ruari was capable of leaving. He'd prove he was more than capable.

"Aedan," he said, wiping the sweat from his brow from the short walk. "I'd prefer to handle this myself." He'd never admit it to his brother, but he was in worse shape than he'd guessed. Perhaps he needed more guards.

"Like you did when you came back near death? I wasn't sure you'd survive this one. Is Munro the guilty party?"

"Aye, in a way. He never touched me, but he ordered his men to beat me. I tried to call him to a man-to-man swordfight, but he refused. I had hoped to uncover something as proof of his black heart, but I failed. Nonetheless, it's my right to go after the fool. I will gladly accept some help. Seems you're correct on that," Ruari admitted sheepishly.

His brother's face creased into a frown. "You shouldn't

be out of bed, Ruari. Jennie said you needed another three days to recover."

"Juliana is leaving by midday and I have to stop them. I wish to make her my wife and she has already accepted my suit. I'll not relent."

Neil, standing beside Aedan as always, was quick to interject. "And you handled your last attempt to gain her hand brilliantly. Will you never learn, *laddie?*"

Ruari had listened to years of criticisms and barbs from this man, but suddenly he'd had enough. He grabbed his brother's second-in-command by the throat. "Keep your thoughts to yourself and stop interrupting me while I'm speaking with my brother."

To his surprise, Neil laughed. "'Tis about time you got some bollocks on you."

"Put him down," Aedan said, although he didn't sound angry. "At least your last move convinced me of your feelings for the lass. I'll agree to send twenty guards with you so you can catch her sire before he leaves to plead your case."

"Many thanks," Ruari said as he pushed Neil away and hurried toward the stables, moving as fast as his injuries would allow him. At least he'd gained no broken bones from his beating.

"Ruari!" His brother's voice echoed across the courtyard.

He spun around briefly but continued to move backward. "What?"

"Try not to get yourself killed this time. You are my only brother."

Ruari couldn't promise that at all.

CHAPTER TWENTY-ONE

———————◆———————

JULIANA'S EYES BURNED WITH UNSHED tears as she rode along. The conversation she'd overheard earlier tormented her. Before they'd left the abbey, her sire and Munro had gone off to talk to the abbey guards about the safest way to travel back with a possible storm coming. They'd left her and Winnie with Munro's men, who'd acted as if she didn't possess ears.

"Haven't seen the Cameron's brother around, have we?" one of them had said in an undertone.

His friend barked out a guffaw, then said, "Nay, we took care of him for a while."

"He was more of a fighter than I thought. He was a fool to think he could convince our laird to give up such a beauty. I'd like to slip between her legs myself."

"Shut your mouths," another warned. "If Aedan Cameron wishes, he could flay all of us."

The first guard, the chatty one, scoffed and said, "Aedan Cameron doesn't have the bollocks to come after us."

One that hadn't said a word yet said, "But if his brother were able, he'd storm over with two dozen Cameron guards and beat you all for what you did to him."

"You had a hand in beating him, too," the guard cajoled.

"Not the way you did. Your blow nearly killed him."

Juliana had bitten her lip to keep from crying out. She'd thought about riding away from them, but they would have caught her. If she wanted to help Ruari, she'd have to figure out another way, although she had no notion of what she could do.

At least she knew he hadn't abandoned her, and he was still alive, from what they'd said, although she hated the thought that he'd been hurt because of her.

Munro had swaggered over then to give his instructions to his guards. Everything had been a whirlwind after that. Joan had come out to say goodbye, and Juliana had hugged her close, doing her best not to shed any tears. The oddest thing had happened then. Joan had whispered in her ear, "Do not worry. I'll take care of everything."

There was no time to ask her what she meant. Her sire had moved them along, Munro guards and all, and an aching void had opened in Juliana's chest.

They traveled for over two hours with no incidents at all. They had stopped for a break when a sound caught her ears, and she turned to see the source.

A lone horse came straight at them. To her surprise, she recognized the rider as her sister. Joan had a wild expression on her face, and for a moment Juliana thought she'd come to scoop her up into the saddle, but instead of heading toward the spot where Juliana stood with her sire, she rode hard for the group of guards talking with Munro.

The rest happened as if in slow movement. Joan leaped from her horse with a screech, directly toward Ailbeart Munro, her arm outstretched. That's when she noticed the reflection off the metal in the sun.

Joan held a dagger in her hand, and it was aimed at Ailbeart Munro's heart.

"Nay," Juliana screamed, running toward her sister, so afraid she'd be hurt. The rest happened in a matter of seconds. Joan's dagger embedded in the flesh of Munro's shoulder. He reacted with a roar, as did his guards. Two guards wrestled her away from Munro, easily taking her weapon from her, but the bastard pulled a dagger from inside his tunic and buried it in Joan's belly.

"Joan!" Her cry came out in a screech.

So many raised voices filled the clearing, but her attention was solely on Joan. She raced to her sister and gathered her bleeding body into her arms. Blood spurted from Joan's belly, and even as Juliana tried to stem the bleeding, she knew it was a lost cause.

Joan clutched Juliana's mantle, her mouth trying to form words, but she couldn't. Juliana set her carefully on the ground so she could apply pressure to Joan's wound, something she'd learned from Ruari's niece.

"Joan, nay. Why did you do that? Nay! I cannot lose you." She sobbed as she watched the life fade from her sister's eyes. "Why, Joan? Why? I could have found another way. I hadn't given up. Joan, don't you give up either. You can't leave me. *Please.*"

Her sister tried to tell her something, but she couldn't understand her words. She put her ear to Joan's mouth, and still, she could only make out occasional words.

"Please...go back to the abbey...vows...letters."

And the light went out of her sister's eyes.

Juliana screamed and screamed and screamed, her arms wrapped around her sister's body as she rocked back and forth like a wee bairn.

———◆———

Ruari and his guards finally caught up near a burn. It was a logical place for them to have stopped, but he knew at once something was wrong.

He heard the screaming as he approached.

Then he saw the blood and the chaos.

His gut clenched as he prayed the woman he loved had not been hurt. "Juliana!" he shouted, hoping to be heard over the din as he jumped off his horse.

He shoved guards out of his way until he reached the middle of the group, then he tried to process the horrible scene before him.

Juliana knelt on the ground next to her sister, who was covered in blood.

She lifted her head and screamed and screamed, a desperate, mournful sound that ripped his soul to shreds.

What the hell had happened?

When he reached her, he saw that her sister was dead, or nearly so. He could do nothing for Joan, and so he had to do what he could for Juliana. He gently freed her hands from her sister's gown, then lifted her into his arms and carried her away from the group. Her father had staggered over, meanwhile, and he fell to the ground next to Joan, while Munro cursed the woman for having sliced him somewhere.

What the hell had happened?

He carried Juliana away from the melee, getting her somewhere where she could hear *his* voice and his voice only. Although the Munro's guards attempted to stop him, Aedan's men held them back easily. "Sweetling, hush, hush," he crooned, trying to get through her hysteria. "Juliana, 'tis me, Ruari. The one who loves you. You remember me? I look a sight, but 'tis me."

She stared up at him, gripping his tunic, and finally stopped screaming. Reaching a hand up to cup his cheek, she asked, "Ruari, what happened? My sister is dead. How could that be?" Her voice was so soft and small, he wished to take all her pain and suffering from her. "Tell me 'tis not true. It cannot be. I held her in my arms while she took her last breath. Oh, Joan. Oh, my dear sister…"

He sat down on a fallen log and settled her on his lap away from the crowd. He motioned to Padraig, not far from them, to keep everyone away from them until he could form a better understanding of the situation.

"Can you tell me exactly how it happened, Juliana?"

She sniffled, still clutching his tunic, but nodded her head. "Joan…Joan…she came at us from behind. She stopped her horse and swung her dagger at Ailbeart…caught him in the shoulder…" Her breath hitched three times as she stared over his shoulder, looking back toward the place where it had happened.

A quiet calm came over her, but raw fury filled her gaze—something he'd never seen in her before. "He did it," she whispered. "Munro took out his own dagger and struck her in the belly. His men had already pulled her away from him, but he didn't care. He stabbed her, pulled the knife out, and cleaned it on her dress. Cold. He was so cold when he did it, as if he hated her, hated *me*. I grabbed her…I don't recall much else until she died in my arms. Oh, Ruari," she said, her voice shaking. "It was awful. I've lost my sister." Her head fell on his shoulder and she sobbed, her whole body shaking with the force of it. He didn't know what else to do but hold her.

Her father appeared in front of him. "Juliana, you must go with him. He's leaving now."

She stared at the man in open disbelief. "Father, how could you even suggest such a thing? I will never marry that man."

At least he had the grace or sense not to argue with her. Juliana's next words shocked Ruari to his core.

"Papa, Joan wished for me to take my vows. Those were her last words to me. Take me home. I'll gather all my things and return to the abbey. I wish to be a nun."

———————

Poor Ruari. He and his guards had escorted Juliana and her sire back to Clavelle Manor, but her father had forced him and his men to sleep outside. Ruari had convinced her that he didn't care, he was just concerned for her.

She knew he still wished to marry her. She wanted that too, but the memory of Joan's face, twisted with pain, was enough to convince her otherwise.

Two mornings after Joan's death, she packed her things

and brought them into the great hall. The time had come
to return to Lochluin Abbey and do as she had promised.
Her sire sat by the hearth, brooding, smelling of whisky.
A cask of it sat on the table beside him.

"So this is it, then," he said. "You're off to desert me
like your sister did. Make me look like a fool to Ailbeart
Munro. He already paid me good coin for you, and if you
choose to become a nun, I'll have to give it back."

"Papa, did you spend that coin?"

"Nay. I still have it all."

"Then give it back," she said in disgust. Was his coin
worth more to him than his two daughters had been?

"Nay. I deserve a portion of it. I'm not giving it back
after all he's done to me." Her father's fist slammed down
onto the table and she jumped at the violence of it. But she
did not intend to back down. Not anymore. He was hiding
something about Laird Munro, she knew it, and the time
had come for him to tell her. After what had happened to
Joan, after what had nearly happened to her, she deserved
to know.

"This is about that night, is it not?" she asked "The night
when I was eight and I woke up because I heard Joan
crying. Laird Munro did something to her, didn't he? Tell
me, Papa. I'm not a wee lass anymore. I want to know what
happened!"

"Naught happened that you need to know about," he
yelled back.

"Tell me!"

Dead silence fell between them, but she would not let
this go. He had to be honest.

In a low voice, she said, "Papa, Joan is *dead*. Tell me what
happened that night."

Her father broke into tears and his head hung as he
sobbed. The only time she'd ever seen him cry like this
was after her mother passed on. But she couldn't stop...
She needed the truth.

He picked his head up and wiped his tears on a nearby linen square. "I'll tell you, even though I swore the truth would go to my grave with me."

She waited, giving him the time he needed.

He cleared his throat, mopped his eyes, and began the tale. "Ailbeart Munro took your sister's maidenhead. She was carrying their bairn, and I told her she had to marry him. When he found out, he was ecstatic. They were to marry three days after that night. But she refused."

She moved over to the chair and slid into it, unable to believe what she'd just heard. "He was to marry Joan?"

"Aye, but she refused. Said she hated him and wished to be a nun."

Something dawned on her. "But the bairn…I have a niece or nephew somewhere? Where is her baby?"

Her sire reached over and clasped her hand. "She lost it soon after she went to Lochluin Abbey. She was there a year before she took her vows."

Her father stared into space over her head.

"When I think about what she did, trying to kill Munro for you, I realize mayhap she lost her mind many moons ago, and the abbey hid it from us."

She reached for his hands on the table, covering them with her own. "Papa, why did you not tell me? Why didn't Joan tell me? I don't understand." Tears began anew and she made no attempt to stop them.

"Because it was just too painful."

Memories of what Joan had said about men pawing at women bloomed in her mind. She wouldn't have said such a thing, she wouldn't have hated him so, if she'd lain with him of her own free will. So he'd taken her innocence from her.

Juliana's hatred for Ailbeart Munro took on a whole new meaning.

CHAPTER TWENTY-TWO

R UARI HAD HOPED JULIANA WOULD come
around. That she would consider marrying him after
all. They returned to Lochluin Abbey, without her sire, and
laid her sister's body to rest on sacred ground. Her father
had said it was just too painful for him to go along.

Ruari had thought that strange, but he didn't ask any
questions. He stayed by Juliana's side during the ceremony,
doing whatever she asked of him.

Hoping she'd come back to him.

It was nearly dark that night when the mourners, mostly
other nuns, left to go to their chambers. The abbey was full
because many had come from Stonecroft Abbey to express
their sympathies.

Her sister had been well-loved.

When the great hall was nearly empty, Juliana stood from
her seat at one of the trestle tables and held out her hand.
"Will you take a walk with me?" She gave him a small
smile.

"Of course. Any time we spend together pleases me."

She led him out to the herb garden and they strolled
hand in hand up and down the neat rows, the half-moon
casting enough light for them to see the path that lay
ahead. "Ruari Cameron, you know I love you."

He didn't like the way she'd made that statement. "As I
love you." He squeezed her hand.

She stopped and stared up at the cloudless sky, the stars luminescent. "You know that when I held my sister in my arms, she tried to tell me something."

"Aye, you've told me what you think she said."

"'Struth. She asked me to return to the abbey, which I think meant Lochluin Abbey, and then she said the words 'vows' and 'letters.' I don't know how else to interpret her words than to think her last wish was for me to take my vows as a nun at Lochluin Abbey."

Regret washed over Ruari. He'd hoped he could convince her that he'd be good a husband. He'd hoped it would be enough to change her mind, but he could see he was wrong.

He leaned his forehead against hers and closed his eyes. "I don't wish to lose you, but I cannot disagree. I don't think 'tis where you belong because I selfishly believe you belong with me. But I cannot interpret her last words any differently than you did."

"I know," she said as she reached up and looped her arms around the back of his neck. She lifted her head and locked her gaze on his. "I will always love you, but I think I must pursue this course. I've talked with Mother Matilda, and she has encouraged me to take my time and be thoughtful about my vocation. She suggested that guilt may be driving me to interpret her words this way, but no one has come up with any other possible meaning. I don't know what else to do other than to think on it. To pray for guidance."

He cupped her cheeks and kissed her, a soft kiss unlike their other passionate kisses. "I'm not happy about it, but I cannot fault you on your decision. 'Tis a preferable choice than being Munro's wife. Promise me something?"

"Anything."

"If you need anything at all, please send a messenger for me. Any time, day or night. I'll not be far away."

"You should find someone else to love," she said softly,

her voice quavering.

"Juliana, we've never spoken about this, but I wish to tell you something. I was married before."

She cupped his cheek, stroking her thumb across the stubble that had accumulated over the course of a long day. "I know. Joan told me. You need not say anything about her. It must have been verra painful for you to lose your wife."

"Aye, 'twas...but we were never..." How could he explain the way it had been between them so she wouldn't think him heartless? "I didn't love her the way I love you. She never loved me. I cannot explain it, but it was verra different. With you—" he reached up and covered her hand with his, "—I wish to have you by my side forever, to look in your eyes in the morn, to kiss you good eve every night. To hold you close and keep you warm on the coldest nights of winter. To make sweet love to you whenever you wish it..."

Even as he said the words, he could see tears misting in her eyes. "Juliana, what I'm trying to say is that you are the love of my life. That much I know. I was gifted with your love for a short time, and for that I am forever grateful. I'll never need another, nor will I want one."

"Nay, you are wrong..."

He frowned. "In what way?"

"I will always love you." She smiled, dropping her hand so she could play with his bottom lip, rubbing her fingers across it. "That will never change. We just cannot marry. Will you visit me from time to time?"

"Aye." He doubted there was aught he could say to change her mind, but Jennie had said something he felt the need to repeat. "I forgot to tell you what Jennie told me about people who are dying, people who know they don't have much time."

"What did she say?"

"Sometimes they can't get the right words out and you

may never know what their last wishes are."

How he wished he could convince her of that.

Instead, he did what he needed to do. He let her go.

——————

Ruari avoided the abbey for the next two weeks, hoping Juliana would have the time she needed to mourn her sister. Hoping she would realize that she wasn't meant to be a nun.

His heart yearned to visit her.

Aedan called him into his solar one day to tell him Munro had paid a visit to the abbey. Apparently, he'd still hoped to convince Juliana to marry him. She'd refused to see him, and he'd gone home in a fury.

"Mother Matilda can be quite a force when she wishes to be," Aedan said. "She can stir up the monks to do her bidding when someone threatens the welfare of one of her charges."

"Why did you not tell me, Aedan? I would have gladly sent the bastard off to his land."

"The abbess sent a messenger in case there was trouble, but I didn't expect any. Juliana's deep in mourning. What a shock for a young lass to hold her sister in her arms and watch her die. I stayed away because I thought it best."

"Mayhap so," Ruari muttered.

"And I feared if I saw the bastard, I'd have a few words with him over how he treated my brother. Fortunately, he left quickly."

Ruari was surprised to see the emotion that crossed his brother's face at the mention of his beating.

"What? You're surprised? Go find a silver platter and check your reflection. You still look like a hideous beast." Aedan chuckled as he gave him a full perusing.

Perhaps Ruari would pretend that was why he'd stayed away from Juliana instead of the true reason.

He was afraid to see her—afraid that she'd tell him she'd

already become a novice. He'd sent a few small gifts to her, a berry fruit tart, soap that smelled of lavender, and a bouquet of wildflowers that smelled just as she did.

While the messenger had always communicated her gratitude, she'd never asked to speak to him.

One day in the lists, he finally lost the drive to fight and tossed his sword onto the ground.

"Lazy arse today, Cameron," Padraig said. "Or is it something else?"

He shook his head, unable to put his frustration into words. His niece Riley walked toward the lists.

"Your answer is coming soon," she said with a smile. Having communicated her enigmatic question, she whirled about like a wee fairy and ran back toward the keep.

"What do you suppose she meant by that?" Padraig asked, scratching his head. "Is your niece always that odd or is she a seer?"

Ruari stared after the lass, her plait bouncing in the air as she ran. "Not a seer that I am aware of, but she's young yet. Mayhap some odd skill is developing inside of her. I must ask Aedan or Jennie about it." He wiped the sweat from his brow with his tunic. "I've had enough for today, Padraig." The truth was his muscles still ached at times from the beating he'd taken.

And the ache in his chest refused to leave him.

"I'm going to visit my mother. I didn't want her to see my face in such a state, but I haven't visited her since the day before I went to Munro's. I've put it off long enough," he said, heading toward the keep. "You stay and keep working our guards. They need the practice."

He strode to the keep and found his mother in front of the hearth in her chamber. "Greetings to you, Mama."

"Ruari, I'm so glad you're here."

He bent down and kissed her cheek and took a seat beside her. "How are your aches and pains today?"

He waited for her reaction to the bruises on his face. It

never came.

"I don't have any aches and pains, but I must tell you that Riley has a message for you."

Puzzled by that, he said, "Riley just gave me a message, but I'm not sure what it means."

"I'm glad she came to see you. Do not worry, you'll find out soon enough. Just remember that I always love you." She smiled and patted his cheek. Her head dipped to her chest, her eyes closing, so he tucked the plaid on her lap around her. "I love you, too, Mama," he whispered as he kissed the top of her head.

He left her there, spoke to the woman who usually kept an eye on his mother, then headed back out into the courtyard in search of Aedan. His brother was walking toward him, a broad smile on his face.

"Aedan, has Mama seemed odd to you?"

"What? Nay. Mama's seemed the same to me, but never mind that. We have visitors and they are here to see you, though I'm uncertain as to why. You'll enjoy their company whatever their message."

His heart sped up at the prospect that Juliana might have come to him, but then his gaze caught the visitors emerging from the stables.

It was Drew Menzie, his wife Avelina, and their four bairns. The Menzies lived nearby, and they were considered family by virtue of the marriage of Jennie's sister to Avelina's brother. The group came toward them, Drew clasping Aedan's shoulder with a wide grin. "Cameron, so nice to see you again. You all fare well? Ruari, my apologies for the trouble you seem to be having, but mayhap your luck is about to change."

He had no idea what that meant so he said nothing.

Avelina, after greeting both of them, said, "Drew, why don't you take the lads out to the lists to observe, while Elyse and I speak with Ruari. Ruari, you remember our lads? This is Tad, the eldest, and the young ones are Tomag

and Maitland." Ruari greeted each of them, but they took
off toward the lists as fast as they could. He guessed the
youngest to be around seven or eight.

"Papa, we're going to find Brin," the lad in back shouted
over his shoulder. The three ran in one straight line, and he
couldn't help but smile.

How he wished he could have had sons of his own. His
mind shifted to Grizella, the old healer who'd stitched his
wound. All this time, he'd wondered why his wife hadn't
become with child. Doirin had told him it was fate—that
it was a sign they weren't meant to have bairns—but all
along she'd been preventing it from happening.

He felt bitterly betrayed.

Word of the visitors must have arrived, because Jennie,
Tara, and Riley burst out of the keep to greet them. Once
the hugging and giggling ended, Avelina said to Jennie,
"We've come to see Ruari. Is there a place we can speak
privately? You are welcome to join us, of course."

Riley boldly took a step forward and announced, "As I
am, correct, Aunt Lina?"

Elyse, whom he guessed to be around six and ten,
stepped forward and touched Riley's cheek. An eerie pause
followed as the two locked gazes. What happened next was
so peculiar, Ruari wouldn't have believed it if he hadn't
seen it with his own eyes. An odd golden glow emanated
from Avelina and jumped first to Elyse and then Riley.

And as quickly as it had come, it vanished.

Elyse broke into a wide smile and said, "Of course, Riley.
I see you are quite special." Jennie's eyes widened, but she
said nothing about the strange aura. She put her hands on
Riley's shoulders and said, "Come inside. Tara and I will
arrange for a light repast while you and Elyse can speak
with Ruari and Riley."

Ruari glanced from one face to the other. Something
odd was transpiring in front of him, but he had no idea
what it meant. He waited for the women to lead the way,

followed by the lasses, then he stepped in behind them.

They were about to ascend the steps into the keep when Riley stopped, twirled around to face him, and said, "You see, Uncle Ruari? 'Tis happening just as I predicted."

CHAPTER TWENTY-THREE

———◆———

JULIANA THREW HERSELF ONTO HER sister's bed and sobbed her eyes out, probably for the tenth time that week. At least she understood all that had happened many years ago, though it raised more questions than it provided answers. Why hadn't her sister confided in her? She'd carried a babe and lost it.

How awful for her. She couldn't imagine how her sister must have grieved the loss of her child, yet she'd never said a word about it.

Everything had been kept secret.

She knew why her sister had been so adamantly opposed to her betrothal to Munro, but why hadn't Joan been more direct with her warnings? Why hadn't she finished telling her about the marriage bed?

No matter how hard she prayed, she had no answers.

Her heart hurt so much that she feared it was beyond repair. She missed her sister, she missed Ruari, and she wished to melt into oblivion. The small, thoughtful gifts Ruari persisted in sending her only made it harder to stay away from him, something she felt she needed to do.

What was she to do?'

She lay on her bed, her head turned to the side, her tears finally spent, though she knew they wouldn't be her last.

Sister Grace knocked on her door and stuck her head inside.

Juliana could barely move her head to speak with her.

"You have visitors, my dear," the nun said with a kind smile. "Please come below stairs." She stepped away as softly and unobtrusively as she had come.

Who would be visiting? The only visitor she could think of was Ruari, so she slipped her toes into her old worn slippers, because she refused to wear the new ones Munro had bought her, and headed down the stairs.

There was no bounce in her step, even for Ruari. If he were here, he would be looking for her to change her mind and agree to marry him, but she couldn't do it yet.

She feared it would dishonor her sister's memory.

When she reached the hall, she was surprised to see a group of unfamiliar people waiting by the hearth. She recognized only two of them—Jennie Cameron and her daughter Riley.

Mistress Jennie greeted her first and said, "I brought two verra special people to see you, Juliana. This is my dear friend Avelina Menzie and her daughter, Elyse."

Avelina was stunning. Tall and willowy, she had haunting green eyes that reminded her of a meadow full of wildflowers. Elyse's hair was long and dark brown, with strange streaks of silver that had nothing to do with age. The color of her eyes was hard to pinpoint. Sometimes they appeared blue, sometimes green, but occasionally they looked golden. She had a warm smile that made her approachable in spite of her strange, striking beauty.

Riley stood behind her, a bit off to the side, her gaze locked on Juliana's. She spoke first, "They've come here for *you*, Juliana."

Mistress Jennie's soft lilting laughter softened Riley's odd comment. "Riley, you'll frighten Juliana. She means they've come to speak with you. Lady Avelina has the gift of sight, and her only daughter has inherited it. They have a message meant just for you, but please sit down, Juliana. How have you been?"

All she could do was shake her head lightly as she stared at them. "I'm not sure. I supposed I'm confused more than anything."

Jennie turned to Avelina and said, "I'm not sure if you know the story, but Juliana lost her only sister Joan about a fortnight ago. Her sister, who was a nun here at the abbey, gave Juliana a message before she passed, and I believe Juliana has been struggling to interpret her message. Am I not right about that, my dear?"

Juliana nodded as she sat in one of the chairs by the hearth, gripping her hands together so tightly that their color was nearly white.

What message could they possibly have for her? She'd never known a true seer before, although she'd heard enough stories not to doubt that they existed.

Lady Avelina dragged over a stool and motioned for Elyse to sit, then settled into the chair closest to Juliana. "I have the gift of sight, but my daughter's gift is much stronger than my own. Elyse has received a message for you from someone, Juliana," she said in a warm, soft tone. "She wasn't sure who was trying to reach out to her, but now that I've heard your story, I'm quite certain 'tis your sister. Elyse will give you the message, and you may choose to do what you wish with it. The dead often leave as a complete surprise, leaving something undone, and I believe 'tis what has happened with your sister."

Tears slid down Juliana's cheeks and she said, "Please go on." She wished to hear the message even though she wasn't sure she believed it was from her sister.

Elyse said, "I'm certain this soul is your sister's. She said she's sorry for how it all turned out, but 'tis for the best."

She couldn't stop the tears from running down her face. "But it isn't."

"Aye, she says everything will be all right as soon as you find what was in her heart. You're confused and you've misinterpreted her. She left a message for you in her chamber. You must find it."

Juliana bolted out of her chair and raced up the stairs, tears blurring her vision so much that she feared she'd trip and fall. Mistresses Jennie and Avelina followed her.

Elyse stood at the base of the stairs and called out, "Stop running. How many times must I tell you, wee sweetie, to stop running all the time?"

Juliana gasped, spun around, and lowered herself onto one of the steps lest she fall. That was exactly what her sister had said to her over and over again when she was a young lass.

Wee sweetie.

"What, Joan? Tell me what to do…please." She stared at Elyse as if she might actually turn *into* Joan.

Elyse shook her head as if coming out of a trance. "She said you'll find her answer in her chamber."

She grabbed her skirts and raced down the long stone passageway until she reached her sister's chamber. Once inside, she collapsed in front of the chest that held Joan's belongings. She forced herself to start looking through it, one item at a time, sobbing as she worked. She'd done this before, though, more than once, and there was nothing.

Jennie and Avelina stood in the doorway, as if uncertain of what to do next, but Elyse circled around them. "Keep searching," she said, joining Juliana in the chamber.

Juliana continued the search, but despair pressed down on her again. Had she come so far only to be pushed backward again?

"Where? Where, Joan? Tell me where. Please."

But Elyse had no further advice to give. Once the chest was completely empty, Juliana hurried over to the shelves at the side of the chamber.

It was then Riley joined them in the chamber. Stepping in past Elyse, she lifted her arm to point at the shelves. "'Tis in the book of letters." Riley's expression was completely blank as she lifted her gaze to Juliana's. "You remember the book of letters I made for you, do you not?"

Juliana rushed to the shelf to grab up the book her sister had prepared for their lessons, which they'd started a few days before Joan died. She brought it back to the bed with her and took a hasty seat, flipping through the pages in the hopes something would jump out at her.

Elyse approached her and took the book from her hands, lifting it and giving it a weak shake. To Juliana's amazement, a piece of parchment fell toward the floor.

Juliana caught the parchment before it landed. She opened it and looked at all the letters carefully inscribed in neat rows. "But I cannot read," she declared to all those around her.

She noticed Mother Matilda now stood behind Mistress Jennie and Mistress Avelina in the doorway.

Avelina walked over to the bed and sat down beside her. "I'd be happy to read it to you, if you don't mind. Do you want the others to listen, or would you prefer for them to leave?"

"I don't care. Is it from my sister?"

Avelina glanced over the parchment. "Aye, 'tis a note from her to you." She set her hand on Juliana's back and said, "Shall I read it now?"

"Aye, please," she whispered, her heart beating as fast as a rabbit's. She was about to hear her sister's last message for her.

Avelina began:

My dearest Juliana,

I have a hard time expressing myself, but I must tell you what is in my heart.

Do not marry Ailbeart Munro. He is a cruel, uncaring man. I know because I nearly married him. Trust me in this and ignore what Papa says.

After praying on the matter, I don't think taking your vows is right for you. You have given Ruari Cameron your heart and he is a good, honorable man. Marry him and I hope you will have many bairns with him.

I have tried to tell you this, but I find the words difficult to say because the truth is I always wanted this for myself, but it didn't happen.

It is my hope that someday you will be happy and have many bairns.

Mama would have wanted this for you.

I want this for you.

I love you with all my heart. I must teach you to read before I can give this to you, but I have at least written my thoughts down. I have this odd feeling that I must write them down, though I know not why.

You will be a wonderful mother someday.

Someday, I'll tell you my other secret, but that is for another day.

Your sister,

Joan

Elyse, who'd returned to the doorway while her mother was reading the letter, smiled at her. A wide, familiar smile like the ones Joan had given her when she was small, "And now I must go, wee sweetie. Be happy."

Jennie and Riley left with Elyse, but Avelina wrapped her up in a tight embrace, and she sobbed into her arms.

CHAPTER TWENTY-FOUR

R UARI WENT TO RETRIEVE HIS own horse a short time after seeing Jennie and the others to the stables, but Aedan stepped in his path.

"Where are you going?"

"I'm going to see Juliana. If they have a message for her, I wish to hear it. I've given them enough time to speak with her privately, but I want to be with her if their message was difficult for her to hear."

"You cannot go with them. Juliana is interested in taking her vows." Aedan stood directly in his path, intentionally blocking him from mounting his horse. "I will not allow you to go over there and cloud the lass's mind. She needs to make this decision on her own without any pressure from you."

"Aedan, I am tired of you telling me what to do. I'm your brother, but I'm also a full-grown adult. Don't you trust me to make my own decisions?"

"I'm warning you, if you interfere with what those lasses are trying to do for Juliana, you'll regret it."

"And what can you do to me? You can't let me go from my position because you haven't given me one. You sound like Mama, thinking I'm too young to do anything. If you'll recall, I'm a man eight and twenty. But then again, mayhap you'll threaten to *banish* me."

Ruari pushed past Aedan and retrieved his horse. He

mounted and rode for the gates.

"Ruari, if you ignore my warning, I *will* banish you from Cameron lands!" Aedan shouted after him. "Don't push me. I will do it!"

He turned his horse around, leaped down, and charged over to his brother, giving him a shove. "There. I pushed you. Now what?" He was so tired of being belittled or ignored by his brother. He'd had enough. "What are you going to do about it, Aedan?"

"You want my worst? Fine! You're banished. Leave and never come back."

Ruari paused to catch his breath, his hands on his hips. "I guess I just learned your true feelings for me, brother."

Aedan's cheeks were dark red, and he could see how upset he was just by the clenching of his jaw. But it didn't stop his brother from speaking his mind. "I do this because I care about you. I don't want to see you throw your life away. Haven't you ever wanted more? You roam around like a lost dog. Now you've had a nice conversation with a beautiful lass, and suddenly you want to incite a clan war? Force the nuns to hate you? What is your purpose in this? It took Jennie and me months to fall in love, to know we were right for each other. After one or two conversations, you think you've found your future wife. You are always making rash decisions, and this is another one."

"To hell with you," Ruari mumbled, heading back to his horse. Aedan's words had been like daggers piercing his flesh.

"Don't do this!"

He was about to mount his horse, but he stopped, clarity finally seeping into his soul. "Aedan, you're so old you've forgotten."

"The hell I have."

Ruari threw his arms over his head. "Then why don't you remember what it was like to fall in love?"

"I remember it well, but it doesn't apply to you. It's

happened too fast."

Ruari leaned toward his brother, bellowing at him loudly enough for the monks to hear. "You don't hear me because you refuse to. Listen well. I love Juliana Clavelle with all my heart. Something I thought I was incapable of because of my first marriage. A marriage full of lies. I don't want lies any more. I'm choosing to go after the love of my life, to try to convince her to trust in my feelings. She's lost and she needs me."

Aedan tried to speak, but he shushed him.

"Nay! I don't wish to hear your empty words anymore. I am going after her because I will follow her anywhere. She means more to me than anything. Can't you see?"

His brother stared at him, an odd look on his face.

Ruari turned around slowly and made his way back to his horse. Arguing with his brother was useless. If Aedan truly wished for him to leave, he'd do it, but he was going to see Juliana first. He mounted and reached for the reins, but Aedan called to him.

"Ruari, wait."

He paused, not bothering to look at his brother—only for Aedan to run out to stand in front of his horse.

"Please tell me you're not trying to stop me from leaving. You can't."

Aedan laughed and stared up at the sky. "Nay. I'll not stop you. Look up. Can you not see the moon peeping out between the clouds, even during the day? 'Tis so bright, yet the stars steal its glory. And the more you stare at the night sky, the more bright beacons of light you'll see around the moon. Jennie and I like to compare the differences in the stars based on the shape of the moon."

"This is hardly the time for star-gazing."

Aedan laughed again, then strode over to stand next to his brother's horse, his hand petting the beast's withers. "Nay, 'tis exactly the right time. My thanks for reminding me of all the reasons I fell in love with Jennie Grant. 'Twas a long time ago." He paused, rubbing the horse's muzzle. "Seems I did indeed forget. I apologize for my foolish remarks. You're my brother, and I support you in this. I hope you can convince Juliana to marry you."

Ruari said, "Many thanks, Aedan. I hope to give you good news upon my return."

"You deserve happiness. Godspeed. If you need anything at all, I'm here for you."

He'd told himself Aedan's opinion didn't matter, but the emotion clogging his throat said otherwise. His brother's support strengthened his will.

When he finally made it to the abbey, he left his horse at the stables. Jennie and the young lasses were exiting the abbey as he approached it, and his sister-in-law strode over to speak with him.

"My thanks for not coming until we were done. Juliana needed to hear the message without you as a witness. I asked Aedan to hold you back, although I wasn't sure how he'd do it."

"He came up with a brilliant plan," Ruari said bitterly. "He told me he'd banish me from Cameron land if I interrupted your visit."

Jennie was clearly taken aback by this declaration. "Banish you? He said that?"

"He did at first. We came to a better understanding before I left, but not before there were some unkind words exchanged."

"I'm sorry to hear that," Jennie said, her voice insistent. "Aedan loves you dearly. You are his only brother. He thinks verra highly of you."

"Thank you for saying so, but if he thought highly of me, he would have made me his second long ago. But I've accepted it. After making a big show of arguing, he gave me his support in this endeavor."

"Which endeavor is this? I think I know, but would you mind clarifying it for me?" She gave him a sideways smirk.

"I wish to make Juliana my wife. I love her more than I thought I was capable of, and I'll not be a fool and walk away."

"I wish you much luck, though it may be wise for you to walk away for a wee bit. She may need some time to absorb the information she just received. I think she'll come to the decision you're hoping for, but I'd let her come to that on her own." She kissed his cheek and walked away from him.

"Jennie," he called out after her.

"What is it?"

"I want to support her, to help her through this." He needed to see her—needed it with a ferocity that shocked him. "I'd like to see her."

"I wouldn't go in there just now, Ruari. She was crying and Avelina was with her."

Avelina did have an unusual gift for comforting others.

"I would give her another day or two," Jennie said softly. "Please, Ruari. Come back later. She heard a difficult message and she must sort it out on her own."

He had no idea what was going on in the abbey, but Jennie had never failed him before. She was probably right. Much as he hated to do it, he'd walk away.

Though that simple act was more painful than he ever would have guessed.

———◆———

Two days.

It had been nearly two days since Juliana had learned the truth about her sister's wishes. She'd spoken with the abbess, who'd asked her to spend at least a sennight in contemplation before she made her final decision.

The truth awakened her late in the night, after all the nuns and the abbess were abed.

She needed to speak with Ruari at once.

She crept down the long passageway, removing her worn

slippers so they wouldn't make any noise on the cold stone, then put them on when she stepped into the dark, cool night. Huddling in her mantle, she stood for a moment in front of the abbey, saying a quick prayer for the Lord to guide her to do the right thing.

She took a deep breath and moved forward, heading to the stables, where she promptly ran into two guards, both friends of Ruari's. These were the guards who'd brought her his little gifts.

"Good eve to you. Would either of you be able to escort me to the Cameron keep? I need to advise the Camerons of something."

"Aye," one of them said. "Ruari gave me strict instructions that if you ever needed him, I was to assist you in any way possible. I'll take you there, my lady."

"I'll go along with you," his companion said at once. "I'll advise the others of where we are headed."

She let out the breath she'd been holding as the first guard went off to find a horse for her. Soon they were riding away from the abbey, headed toward Cameron land.

Grateful for that small bit of time, she needed to figure out what she wished to do when she arrived. How did one go about telling a guard to drag Ruari out of bed?

She needn't have worried.

Padraig and Ruari were seated in front of a small hut outside the gates, both drinking ales.

"Ruari?" she said as she stopped her horse. The sight of him lit something inside her, filling her with warmth.

"Juliana? Are you hale? I was coming to see you first thing on the morrow."

The guard spoke up. "She asked to see you. Would you like us to wait for you, my lady?"

"Nay," Ruari said. "My thanks for seeing to her safety. I'll send my own guards to escort her back."

Once the guards left, he moved over to her horse and asked, "Are you sure you are hale?"

"Ruari, I feel free for the first time in a long time. But why are you out here? Do you not sleep in the Cameron keep?"

"Most of the time," he said with a shrug. "This is where Padraig sleeps, so I've decided to join him for a bit." He helped her down and said, "Come inside and I'll find you something warm to drink. No one will know you're here."

"Are you sure?" She peeked around the area, though it was a good distance from the other cottages.

Padraig stood and said, "I'll stay out here and guard you from this chair. You speak with Ruari privately, my lady."

"I won't take but a short bit of his time," she said, then stepped inside the door Ruari held open for her. It was a simple cottage. Two chairs sat in front of the hearth. The flames had died down, but Ruari put more firewood in it, sending sparks shooting into the air. A table and two chairs sat in the middle of the hut, and beyond them there were two beds separated by a chest. A couple of other chests, stacked with various goblets and daggers, completed the furniture.

"Sit, please," Ruari said. It struck her that he sounded nervous, which made her feel less so. "How are you? I knew Avelina, Jennie, Elyse, and Riley visited with you, but I never heard what came of it. Jennie said she thought it was a good visit for you. I wished to come, but Jennie convinced me to give you some time." He moved his chair so it was directly next to hers, then cautiously took her hand. "I hope 'twas helpful."

"Ruari, it was so helpful. I am elated. My sister wanted me to marry you. Your nieces led me to the book where she'd hidden a note for me." She explained how it had all come to pass.

"Truly? And she never told you any of this?"

"Nay. I don't know why she didn't tell me how she felt, but I'm so grateful she left me a message. The abbess asked me to think on it for a sennight, to pray for guidance from our Lord, but I don't wish to wait any longer. If you'll still have me, I wish to marry you."

Ruari jumped out of his chair and tugged Juliana to her feet, wrapping his arms around her. "Lady Juliana," he said, his voice thick with emotion, "would you do me the honor of becoming my wife?"

"Aye! Naught would please me more."

His lips descended on hers, and she sighed, so pleased to be this close to him again. His tongue reached out to hers, encouraging it to dance, and she pressed closer and closer to him, melding her body against his until they nearly felt as one. She stopped and placed her hand on his chest. "When, Ruari? And where will we live? Here on Cameron land? In our own cottage or in the keep?"

Ruari said, "Wherever you would like."

"You have not changed your mind, have you? What is it?" She gave him a puzzled look, surprised by his answer.

"I thought we'd live on Cameron land, but mayhap we should do something special, something different." He pursed his lips and locked his gaze on hers. "Mayhap we'll run away, marry at a kirk, and find our own place to live far from here. I have so many friends in other clans. We could live with the Grants or Ramsays. Perhaps Padraig's brother would have use for me."

"Are you certain? I love the thought of traveling for a time, but don't you have responsibilities to your brother?"

"I have no true responsibilities here, and I'd love to visit with many of my cousins, introduce you to them."

She thought for a moment, considering his words. Although she didn't wish to take him away from his family, he painted an alluring picture. Her father hadn't allowed her to see much of the world. "Could we visit them each and see which we'd like best? I have not traveled much. I would love to go into the Highlands or anywhere new. It would be like an adventure, our verra own adventure as husband and wife."

He hugged her close and rested his chin on the top of her head. "We'll be so happy. I have plenty of coin saved."

"When shall we leave? Are you sure you don't wish to marry here?"

"Nay, I don't wish to burden my brother. It is my second marriage, so a quiet ceremony suits me fine. We'll have a celebration upon our return. I need to gather my things and say my farewells to my mother, Padraig, and a few others. You gather your sister's things and pack a satchel. I'll bring an extra horse to carry our things, and we'll go off on our own."

She hugged him tight. "I love you, Ruari."

"I love you, my sweetling. I cannot wait to make you my wife."

It finally felt like her life was going the right direction. Only one thing bothered her. Her sister's secret. "Could I make a request? I would like to see my father before we leave. My sister shared a secret with me. I want to ask him about it. And I would like to tell him of our marriage."

"Agreed, but not until after we marry. I fear he'll attempt to change your mind."

"Never." She leaned against him and kissed him again.

"The day after the morrow. Break your fast, and I'll come for you just before the sun is highest."

"I'm so excited," she giggled, jumping up and down a bit. "Seal it with a kiss?"

They did indeed seal it with a passionate kiss, one she felt all the way down to her toes.

She was to be the wife of Ruari Cameron. This time naught would stop her.

CHAPTER TWENTY-FIVE

A LTHOUGH RUARI HAD SETTLED HIS differences with Aedan, he was pleased with the plan he'd made with Juliana—a plan he didn't intend to share with anyone but Padraig.

Perhaps he'd find a purpose with one of his cousins. He'd known for some time he wasn't needed on Cameron land.

One more day, and he'd be leaving. He headed toward the tower room to see his mother, opening the door quietly in case she was asleep. She sat in front of the hearth, staring into the flames, her needlework abandoned on her lap.

"Ruari! I'm so glad you're here. Sit with me a bit?" She pointed to the chair next to her. "I'm lonely this morn. No one has been in to see me."

"Didn't Brin stop? Or Tara and Riley?"

"Oh, they're all busy. How do you fare? You have not been sickly, have you? I haven't seen you for a few days."

"I'm hale, Mama. I've just been busy. Listen, I may be gone for a few weeks. Don't worry. I'll be back to visit with you," he said, glancing over his shoulders to make sure no one listening.

"Ruari, when will you stop comparing yourself to Aedan? I see you looking for him. You're a fine lad, too. The stars determined who would be the stronger. Aedan was my first born, so he is the leader and also the strongest. You need not let it upset you any longer."

"Mama, I don't. I accept Aedan as my laird. Why do you keep saying that to me?" How he wished he could convince her to stop comparing him to Aedan.

"Oh, Ruari. I know how you think. You should go out to the lists to practice. I'm cold. Will you find another fur for me, please?"

He found two furs, tucked them around her shoulders, then kissed her forehead and left, still pondering why his mother felt the need to repeatedly mention that Aedan was the stronger brother. He hated that word. He'd made himself stronger than Aedan long ago by working so hard in the lists, but his mother hadn't seemed to notice.

Padraig greeted him in the hall. "Any change in plans? Everything arranged so far?"

"Aye, I only need to collect my coin for the journey. I'm going to do that now, then I'll bring my satchel down to our hut." He climbed the stairs to his chamber, then split his coin into two drawstring bags—one small one to carry on his person and one large one to bring in his satchel. When he finished packing, he carried it outside to hide it in Padraig's hut. Only he didn't make it very far. Just before he strode through the gates, a small voice called out to him.

Riley.

His dear niece raced toward him, her legs flying across the grass near the portcullis. "Uncle Ruari?"

"Good morn to you, Riley. Is something wrong?"

She stopped in front of him, a brilliant smile lighting up her face, but only for a brief moment. Her face turned deadly serious. "Uncle Ruari, you must go."

He had no idea what she meant, so he knelt down in front of her so they were face-to-face. "Sweetie, what do you mean by that?"

"You must go. I've been told to tell you so."

Her face was so serious for one so young that he didn't know whether or not to believe her. But according to Juliana, Elyse and Riley were the ones who'd conveyed

Joan's message from beyond the grave. He'd be a fool to discount what she had to say.

"Go now, please."

Ruari thought he'd do best to handle the matter delicately. "I believe you, but where shall I go?"

"It does not matter. Ride your horse off Cameron land, and they will lead you."

"They? Who are they?" An eerie feeling crept up his back.

She twirled around and ran back toward the keep.

He changed his direction and headed for the stable first to saddle his horse. The stable lad noticed him coming, so he readied his stallion and walked him out to him.

Ruari's mind flew in a dozen different directions. He prayed Juliana wasn't in trouble, but who else could it be?

He mounted his horse after settling his satchel behind the saddle. The lad asked him where he was going, but he ignored the question.

How could he answer when he didn't know?

Tugging the reins, he sent his horse into a gallop, heading off Cameron land toward the abbey, but then he felt the sudden urge to veer toward the south.

He didn't know why, but he didn't ignore it.

A short time later, he had his answer. A group of riders, about a dozen, were headed south with a prisoner in their midst, his hands tied behind his back.

Neil.

Neil had been taken prisoner by a group of Munro guards and they were headed south toward Munro land. Ruari immediately went into spy mode, because this time he was wise enough to know he couldn't take on a dozen men. He led his horse into the forest while the riders stayed on the main path. He could follow them in this manner for at least two hours, which would bring him almost to Munro land.

As he rode, his mind shifted to Juliana and their plan to

leave on the morrow. Should he shift the responsibility of saving Neil to his brother? Aedan could pursue this group with plenty of guards.

No. There was no doubt in his mind. If he didn't continue his pursuit, Neil's life might be forfeit.

Although Neil was a thorny bastard and they had their issues, he needed to do the right thing.

They were nearly on Munro land when he overheard a conversation that tore his insides apart.

"Did they get the lass?" one guard said.

"Aye, they had to tie up a few guards, but they got her out. They're about an hour ahead of us," another answered.

"They did not hurt the nuns, did they?" asked a third. "The Munro gave strict instructions to leave the abbess and the sisters unharmed."

The first guard guffawed. "The only feisty one was our soon-to-be mistress. She'll make a fine lady to the Munro. She bit your brother."

"Didn't think it would take three tries for us to finally steal her away."

Ruari's ears pricked over that statement. What the hell were they talking about?

"The first time, they waited too long. They were too close to Cameron land."

"Aye, we lost three men."

"At least your brother survived that one. 'Twas a good thing they didn't wear their Munro plaids."

"Aye. He said he nearly had her when they tried to grab her near Stonecroft Abbey, but the bastard Cameron hid her too quickly. Still, he got a good slice on her sister."

Ruari couldn't have been more shocked. The two attacks had been aimed at Juliana. That bastard Munro had sent his men after her, likely to avoid paying whatever dowry he'd agreed upon with her sire. Thank the Lord that they'd been able to save her from kidnapping the first two times.

The louts continued their conversation about their dirty deeds, chuckling all the while. Ruari wished to kill the bastards for touching his betrothed.

But he couldn't attack them before he knew what he was walking into. He had to find out where they were keeping her.

The riders traveled across the bridge with a loud enough clatter that he knew the portcullis protecting the Munro keep had been lifted. He stopped his horse at the edge of the dense forest looking over the castle and its wall. He'd have to scale it or find an entrance around the back.

Or perhaps there was a tunnel underneath the keep.

As he was mulling over his choices, a voice startled him from behind.

"Do not even consider going in on your own."

Padraig.

He'd never been so pleased to see someone. He clapped his cousin on the back and said as much.

"Who are you after now?"

He lost his smile as quickly as he'd gained it. "I came after Neil, but I overheard the guards discussing Juliana. She was stolen from the abbey an hour before they kidnapped Neil."

"Neil? Kidnapped? Or was he willingly traveling with them?"

"He was tied up," Ruari replied, his gaze still taking in everything about the Munro keep. "I also learned it was Munro's men who tried to steal Juliana away twice. They dressed up like reivers."

"Truly? Munro tried to kidnap her outside the abbey?"

"Aye, I heard his men having a chortle over it. They were also responsible for the attack on the way to Stonecroft. Both were attempts to kidnap Juliana."

"Hellfire. That explains much. Except...why the hell would Munro want Neil? Juliana, I understand, but why would he want to kidnap that salty bastard?"

"I have no idea," he said, finally shifting his gaze to meet Padraig's eyes. "But I intend to find out."

CHAPTER TWENTY-SIX

JULIANA STRUGGLED NOT TO SOB uncontrollably, but she didn't want to give Munro the satisfaction. Ten Munro guards had stolen her from the great hall of the abbey, whereupon she'd been tied up and tossed onto a horse.

It only comforted her a wee bit that she'd spat at, kicked, and scratched several of the guards. She'd even bitten one.

When the guards had pushed her into the Munro's great hall, he'd been awaiting her with a smile. "My lady, 'tis lovely to see you again."

"Set me free," she'd barked at him, but to no avail.

"Sorry, my dear, but you'll be marrying me on the morrow. You don't wish to stay?" he'd asked, his eyes turning nearly black. He wore his gray plaid and a tunic—his regal appearance a mockery of the cruel man she knew him to be.

"Nay, I wish to marry Ruari Cameron, not you." The Munro great hall was quite stark compared to the warm Cameron hall. Not a single tapestry hung in this hall, and the only decoration was a pair of swords crossed over the hearth.

Worse yet, the rushes were quite disgusting. Not quite what one would expect from a laird's holdings.

The Munro looked at her for a long, drawn-out minute, his gaze cruel and challenging, then announced, "Take her to my mistress's chamber. Lock the door." He'd walked away as the guards grabbed ahold of her and carried her up the staircase.

She'd kicked and bit two more.

The chamber they'd locked her in had clearly been decorated for a lady. A tub was pushed up against the wall, and there were fine soaps and dried flowers everywhere. Although the bed was small, it was in much better condition than the great hall.

She paced the chamber, wondering how long it would be before word reached Ruari that she'd been stolen away. They'd tied up all the nuns and the guards, though they hadn't hurt any of the women, fortunately.

The only hysterical one had been Sister Grace.

Loud voices reached her ear. It struck her that her chamber was just off the top of the stairs, so it would be possible she was overhearing people talking in the great hall.

"Talking" was a kind word for the bellowing she listened to.

She held her breath as she pressed her ear to the wood, her hands resting against the solid frame. When she could finally hear the voices clearly enough, she gasped and almost jumped back from the door.

One voice was her sire's.

She whimpered but forced herself to continue listening.

"I want my coin back, Clavelle. You owe me."

"The hell I do. You killed my eldest daughter…my sweet Joan."

"She stabbed me first, or have you forgotten that fact? It was self-defense. Not a single sheriff in all of England would fault me for that. I want the coin I paid you. You promised me one of your daughters."

"Why? You're still marrying her. I deserve it."

"I have to force her to marry me, no thanks to you. She's headstrong, and 'tis all your fault for rearing her badly."

She heard nothing but silence now between the two.

The silence had lingered for an uncomfortably long time. Oh, how she wished she could see their expressions.

"Clavelle, I'll allow you to keep the coin under one condition."

Juliana's eyes widened at that comment. She held her breath again, pushing her ear against the door so hard that she feared she'd leave a mark on her skin.

"Name it. If I can, I will," her father said.

"Tell me where he is."

At least she thought that was what Munro had said—she couldn't hear clearly.

"Where who is?"

"My son."

"Your son?" her sire's voice grew louder. "What son?"

"The son your daughter gave birth to in the abbey. I know all about him! He's nearly two and ten. I want him here now."

"What? I know not of what you speak. Joan had a son? Nay…nay…if she did, they would have told me. My wife said the bairn died the day after she went to the abbey."

"'Tis a lie. He lived!"

"Who told you this? I know naught of a grandbairn's existence."

"One of the guards at the abbey said he had information for me. It cost me a sack of coin, but he told me Joan gave birth to a laddie and they sent him away. Where is he? I want to know, and if I have to beat it from you, I will."

"Nay, nay! 'Tis all a lie. Margery would have told me. She would have. She…"

Her sire's sobs echoed through the hall, a sound that tore at her heart. Tears slid down her own cheeks.

Was this the secret Joan had referred to in the letter?

Did she have a nephew alive somewhere?

"I have to go inside and see where she is," Ruari said. "I can get her out and go back for Neil later."

"Heed my words, Ruari. You'll not be any help to her if you run off by yourself. Your spy tactics have gotten us here, but how do we get them out?"

A rustling in the bushes behind them had them both unsheathing their weapons. But when the culprit emerged, Ruari was surprised to recognize him.

Aedan had both palms held up. "I know you might like to skewer me, Ruari, but not yet. Please."

"Hell, the best way to get yourself skewered is to sneak up on someone who has a sword," Ruari said, putting his weapon away.

"Never mind that. Tell me what you've learned."

"Juliana and Neil are being held against their will by Laird Munro. I'm sure we can guess why he wants Juliana, but why Neil?" Aedan shook his head, indicating he was as baffled as they were by Neil's inclusion in the scheme.

"We haven't figured out why Neil is here. But we did learn it was Munro's men who attacked us outside the abbeys, both times."

Aedan shook his head in wonder, scratching his beard. "Bastard."

"How did you know to come after us?" Padraig whispered to Aedan.

"Riley. She told me about her premonition, so I decided to bring some men and help."

"I would never have known to come here if not for her," Ruari said. "I don't know what to make of her skills."

Aedan sighed and wiped the sweat from his brow. "'Tis what happens when you marry a healer. She's just learning about her gifts, but I have a feeling they'll continue to grow."

"How many men have you?" Ruari pressed.

"Thirty. How many does Munro have?"

"Probably forty or fifty. I'm going inside to see if I can

free Juliana on my own once it's dark. Or at least to figure out where the two of them are being held. Another half hour or so, and I should be able to sneak in." He rubbed his beard, scratching his chin. "Why the hell is Neil in there? Aedan, have you missed something? You must have an inkling about it."

"I don't, but he and I have not been seeing eye to eye of late." He paused, then added, "I'd like you to be my new second when this is over." He clasped his shoulder. "You've impressed me with your skills of late."

They were words he'd longed to hear for as long as he could remember, but the timing was all wrong. He had to be honest with his brother. "Aedan, I'm honored, but I cannot give you an answer just yet."

Aedan gave him a perplexed look. "I thought this was what you wanted."

"It is." He glanced back at the castle. "Or it was. Juliana is more important to me. I have to get her out. We'd planned to run away and marry, travel to our relatives. I can't answer you until I speak with her."

"So be it."

Padraig cast them both a huge grin.

"What?" Ruari said.

"After all this time, you might turn him down. You're full of surprises, Ruari."

Aedan shook his head, then stared at Padraig. "How did you get to be such a wise arse? Your parents must pull their hair out over you."

His grin showed all his teeth. "They've been known to do so."

Ruari looked at the two in bafflement, then asked, "Why aren't you asking Padraig to be your second? I figured 'tis why you brought him here."

"Padraig? Hell nay. He was making his sire daft, and his brother wants him to be his second. He's been growing his guards and wants to put someone else in charge of them."

Padraig's grin disappeared. "He does?"

"'Tis what I was told. When I feel you're ready, I'm to send you to your brother Roddy. There's only one problem."

"What problem?" Padraig's shocked expression made Ruari almost laugh aloud. He knew what was coming next.

"I told your sire you'll never be ready. You're too much of a wise arse."

A sudden bolt of lightning shot out across the sky, followed by a loud boom of thunder, enough to shake the ground they stood on.

"Holy shite. We're all about to die," Padraig said, the color draining from his face.

"Nay, 'tis perfect," Ruari said. "The storm will provide me with cover. Once the rain starts, I'm going in around the back. Aedan, ready your men for an attack. You'll know when. Padraig?"

His cousin couldn't stop staring at the lightning scissoring across the sky.

He grabbed his tunic and said, "You're coming with me."

CHAPTER TWENTY-SEVEN

———◆———

JULIANA JUMPED WHEN THE FIRST bolt of lightning hit, followed by a boom of thunder. She had to get out. That was the only thing on her mind. She opened each chest, looking for any weapon she could find, but there was nothing of use.

Nothing except for the dagger from Joan, which she still had in her pocket.

To her surprise, the door flew open and her sire stood before her. "Juliana, run. Go to the kitchens and out the back entrance. I'll keep Munro inside. He's gone daft."

Juliana didn't hesitate, pausing only to kiss her sire's cheek as she ran out the door into the passageway. Her sire pointed toward the back staircase, so she flew in that direction, her worn slippers making too much noise as she pounded down the steps. She pushed through the door to the kitchens, then headed straight out the back, ignoring the shouts of the cook and the kitchen helpers.

Rain pounded down on her, but she plunged ahead, dipping her head down to protect her face from the torrential downpour. She found the door in the back of the curtain wall, tugged on it until it opened, then fled as fast as she could.

She screamed as she lost her footing on a hill at the back, something she hadn't expected. Sliding and screaming, she rolled and catapulted down the slippery slope until she hit the bottom with a thud. Her hand hit something hard enough that she feared she'd broken a bone, but she pushed against it, forcing herself to a standing position. The ground was covered in water, flooding nearly to her ankles, but she raced across the landscape, never stopping.

"Juliana, come back or I'll kill you! If I cannot have you, no one will." Ailbeart's voice carried through the storm, but she ignored him, plowing ahead through the mud and water, tripping again on something sticking out of the dirt. She landed hard and her head hit something. Maybe a tree root, although it felt too hard.

Moaning, she rolled over onto her back, opening her eyes and brushing the wet strands of hair out of her face. She tried to push her way to her feet, but then she saw it.

And she screamed and screamed and screamed.

She'd tripped over a bone and hit her head on a skull sticking out of the ground.

Bones were everywhere. Bolts of lightning lit up the entire area.

She was in the middle of an unmarked graveyard.

Running straight toward her was Ailbeart Munro, a snarl on his face. His hands were over his head, wielding a dagger. "He'll not have you."

That dagger was aimed directly at her.

CHAPTER TWENTY-EIGHT

RUARI HEARD A SCREAM AS he rounded the back of the curtain wall, and he instantly knew it was Juliana. He took off toward the scream, but then found himself hurtling down a steep hill, only visible because of the lightning that lit up the area in flashes.

"Padraig, go back! Go for Aedan."

He managed to keep his feet underneath him, scrambling for anything to keep him upright.

Juliana's scream echoed through the night, a sound as tortured as anything he'd ever heard. He hurried toward her, stumbling over rocks and broken branches until he saw her lying on the ground with her head tipped back in a violent scream.

Another flash of lightning illuminated a body in the dark aiming straight for her.

Reaching Juliana moments before her attacker did, he shoved her behind him and unsheathed his weapon. Ailbeart Munro bellowed gutturally as he tried to strike him with his dagger, but Ruari drove his sword into the man's belly, ending his life in an instant.

He reached for Juliana and lifted her into his arms, tucking her close to his chest, screams continuing to rip from her chest as she clutched his wet tunic.

"Hush, lass. I have you now. He'll never bother you again." He kissed her forehead, doing his best to force her gaze upon him.

"Ruari, Ruari, Ruari…"

"I have you. I'll protect you forever."

"Ruari, the bones…there are bones everywhere…I tripped on them, touched them… Get me away from this ghastly place…

Ruari glanced at his feet and turned in a circle. She was right.

He stood in the middle of what appeared to be an unmarked graveyard.

Leading Juliana around the hellish spot, he found an area that wasn't so steep. Fortunately, the rain had let up slightly, allowing him to make his way up past the curtain wall back to where he'd left Aedan.

Padraig reached him first. "She's hale? Where's Munro? They cannot find him."

"She'll be fine," he said, giving her a reassuring squeeze. She was still clutched to his chest. "Who is looking for Munro? He's dead at the bottom of the hill. He tried to kill Juliana."

"Aedan. He took his men inside the gates once we left. He didn't wish to wait apparently. He heard two guards say their laird had gone daft, so he took his men in. No one gave him too much of a fight. Bring Juliana inside."

"Have you found Neil?"

"Aedan is looking for him. Follow me."

Juliana continued to cling to Ruari, clearly in shock, so he kept whispering to her in the hopes it would help her overcome the horrors they'd seen. "Sweetling, I love you. Do you remember we're to marry soon?"

She gave him a small nod, though she kept a death grip on the back of his neck.

"Aye, I love you. He was going to force me to marry him," she said with a shaking voice. "The man who killed my sister."

"Never mind that now. He'll never bother you again.

I'm taking you inside where 'tis warm."

The portcullis was open, and Aedan's men had formed a line at the entrance, waiting to see if any other of Munro's men dared to show up. Several of the men nodded to him as they passed. Others were restraining Munro men, taking their weapons and searching them.

Ruari carried Juliana inside the great hall, bringing her straight to the hearth. He picked a chair and settled into it, cradling her on his lap. Aedan came to his side at once. "Munro?"

"Dead. At the base of the hill behind the curtain wall."

"His men gave up quickly. They weren't too loyal. I've already had several beg to join our clan. Anything else to report?"

"Just that we found an unmarked graveyard in the back. Mighty suspicious. Did you find Neil?"

"He was in the cellars. They're bringing him up now. Once I know whether he's hale, I'll look into the matter of the graveyard."

The hall looked as if a battle had taken place, broken furniture covered the dirty rushes while the Cameron guards herded any men with injuries to the other end of the hall to be tended. The serving lasses were huddled in a corner crying, but the men were doing their best to calm them.

A few moments passed, and Neil finally emerged into the hall. He approached the hearth and sat in one of the open chairs, Aedan behind him.

"You are hale?" Ruari asked.

The man appeared tired and beaten. Ruari had never seen him look older.

He wiped the dirt from his face with his tunic. "I suppose I owe you both an apology."

"What you owe us is an explanation. What did Munro want with you?" Aedan asked, his hands on his hips as he stood over the man.

Ruari didn't often see Aedan as upset as he was at this moment.

Neil held his hand up. "Water? Could I have a drink first? Then I'll explain."

Aedan waved for one of his men to find Neil something to drink, then said, "If Ruari hadn't followed you, we would have had no idea you and Juliana were here. Whatever you did, you put many lives at risk."

Juliana had finally calmed, and she snuggled against Ruari, her head on his shoulder. Her hand lightly rubbed his forearm, as if she were afraid he might disappear. He kissed her forehead and awaited Neil's explanation.

The older man grabbed the ale one of the guards had brought him, took a few long gulps, then finally spoke. "Aedan, I will bow out of my job as your second-in-command as I am no longer worthy of the position. Ruari will make a fine second."

"I'd already offered him the position, Neil. Finish the tale."

He pursed his lips, but he had enough sense not to object. "I fell in love with Juliana's sister, Joan, when I helped escort her to Lochluin Abbey. We became friends, and she confided in me the real reason she was there."

Juliana's sire came up behind them and said, "My daughter was carrying Munro's bairn, but she refused to marry him. She said she hated him." He fell into a nearby chair. "Juliana, I cannot apologize enough for my part in this. He promised to take care of her, and she was carrying their bairn…I had no idea how daft he was."

"Papa, did Joan have a son? I heard you talking with Munro through the door."

"Not that I'm aware of. Your mother told me she lost the bairn."

Neil hung his head, his elbows now on his knees.

"Neil?" Aedan prompted.

He sat up and closed his eyes. "I loved your sister, Juliana."

Dead silence.

"I fell in love with her when I continued to visit with her. Your mother had talked the abbess into keeping her in hiding until she had the bairn. Then she would give it up to someone, but she couldn't do it. When she held her daughter in her arms, she couldn't give her up."

"She didn't have a son?"

Neil leaned his elbows onto his knees again. "She had a daughter, and only the abbess knows where she is hidden. The abbess and one guard who died not long ago. Munro found out I knew something, though I know not how. He thought I knew where his child was being kept, although he thought he had a son, not a daughter, and he attempted to beat it out of me."

Aedan said, "And you hid that secret all these years?"

"Aye, because I promised her."

A look of guilt crossed Neil's face, but it disappeared with a toss of his head. "At least I didn't kill my own wife like your brother did."

Ruari went after Neil, grabbing him by the tunic and hauling his fist back to punch him, but Aedan stopped him.

"What the hell does that mean, Neil? He was nowhere near his wife when she fell off her horse."

Ruari let go of him to allow him to speak freely.

"If he hadn't argued with her, it never would have happened," Neil explained, a glint of satisfaction in his eyes.

Aedan looked at his brother and said, "Now you can hit him."

"With pleasure." He hit him hard enough to knock him down.

And he couldn't help but smile.

———◆———

When they finally arrived back on Cameron land, Ruari still hadn't adjusted to all he'd heard. Nor did he expect Juliana had processed the revelation that she had a niece somewhere.

He kissed her neck because she'd fallen asleep against him. "We're almost there, love," he whispered. "I'll have you in decent clothes soon."

She'd gratefully accepted a gown from one of the serving lasses.

But something niggled at him as they continued on toward a keep.

"Aedan," he called out to his brother next to him. "Do you smell smoke?"

"Aye," he said. They exchanged a look, then both brothers pushed their horses to go faster.

The closer they came to Cameron land, the stronger the scent grew. When they drew close, they noticed a brigade of clan members passing buckets of water along in a line from a well toward the keep. Others ran back and forth in a less organized fashion, shouts of fear and anguish filling the air.

Aedan dismounted so fast, Ruari barely saw him do it.

"Jennie? Tara, Riley…Brin!"

Jennie greeted him swiftly, explaining, "The children are all fine. No one was hurt."

"Where is the fire?" he asked, pushing past Jennie and taking her hand.

Ruari followed him, holding Juliana's hand. She'd awakened enough to dismount on her own and was walking on her own two feet. "Go," she said, squeezing his hand. "I'll wait here. The smoke…"

The smoke was heavier than he'd ever seen from a keep fire. Stone didn't burn easily.

"How did it start, Jennie? Where?" Aedan bellowed, holding his shirt over his face as he drew closer to the smoke. "Is the fire out?"

"Aye, your men put the fire out." She turned into one of the huts. "Your mother, Aedan. She fell asleep and must have set a candle too close to the furs next to the hearth.

We got her out, but she took in quite a bit of smoke. I brought her here so I could keep an eye on her."

She led the brothers to the bed where their mother lay, breathing heavily. "Aedan," she said, reaching for her son. "Go back in. You must get…Ruari…my bairn…"

"Mama, Ruari's right here." Aedan reached for him, pulling him closer.

"Mama, I'm fine. I'm right here." He knelt next to the bed so she could see his face.

Her hand reached for his cheek, but to his surprise, she said, "Nay. Ruari is only ten. He's just a lad. You must get him out."

"Here he is, Mama," Aedan said. "He's fine." Something flashed in his eyes, and his gaze fell to Brin, who'd joined them in the hut. Leaning down to his son, Aedan whispered, "Just tell her you're fine."

"I'm fine," Brin said.

"Mama. Say Mama."

Brin repeated. "I'm fine, Mama."

"Oh, thank the Lord above. Ruari, I was so worried about you. Now you must stop worrying that Aedan is the chieftain and you're not." Her eyes drifted closed.

Jennie patted Brin's back and said, "Well done. You can go back outside. Go to the stables away from the smoke, Brin." He scampered away.

Ruari glanced at his brother, stricken. "Now she's lost her mind?"

Jennie patted his wrist and said, "Her mind has been going for a long time, Ruari. She's in and out. It depends on the day."

Ruari stared at his mother, trying his best to comprehend what this meant.

"You didn't notice?" Aedan asked.

Ruari scratched his head, still staring at his mother lying asleep in the bed. "I knew she was confused at times, but I didn't think she'd lost her mind completely."

"She's considered you to be ten for quite a while," Jennie said. "That often happens with older people. They revert back to their favorite times in their lives. When your father was still alive and you and Aedan were younger. She still loves you." She walked out and said, "I'm going to see if anyone else needs me, Aedan."

Aedan looked at him thoughtfully. "You truly think she thought you less than me as a man?" he asked. "Hell nay. She considered you too young." He grinned at him then, slapping him on the back.

His mother awakened and said, "Ruari, where are you? Ruari, come sit with me."

"You always were her favorite," Aedan continued, although it was said with no umbrage.

Ruari sat on the stool next to the bed and reached for his mother's hand. He didn't say anything, afraid his deep voice would confuse her. He wanted her to think whatever she wished. Whatever gave her comfort.

"That's my lad."

She closed her eyes and fell back asleep.

He stared at his dear mother, wondering why he'd been so blind to her condition. True, she sometimes spoke to him as if he were a wee lad, but he'd only known her to do so after dark. He'd told himself her mind wandered at night, when she was tired.

"I'm so sorry, Mama," leaning over to kiss her cheek. "I should have visited you more often."

He swiped at his eyes, still holding her hand to warm the cool appendage. "All this time, I thought you didn't believe in me. I wrongly accused you of thinking Aedan was the better man. But to you, he was simply the older man."

He stared up at the ceiling, doing his best to stay the tears in his eyes.

"Hell."

He sat there for a long time, staring at his mother's sleeping face, wondering how he could have misunderstood her so.

Then a sudden understanding hit him.
"Because I wanted to."

CHAPTER TWENTY-NINE

RUARI LAY IN BED NEXT to his new wife. He'd never thought it possible to be this happy. He'd told her so many times.

They'd married quietly, though her sire had attended the wedding. He'd returned home immediately afterward, saying he needed to rest after all that had happened.

Especially since they'd learned that the graveyard behind Munro Castle held the bones of Ailbeart's three wives. His three dead wives—something her father had struggled to accept. Although it had taken Juliana some time to overcome the shock of that discovery, the happiness of the past fortnight had helped.

Stirring in bed, she stretched her arms and then reached for him. "Will I ever tire of you, husband? Make love to me."

"Are you sure? You're not sore from last night?"

"Never."

Ruari kissed her tenderly, but she slipped her tongue into his mouth, and soon their tongues were dueling.

He ended the kiss with a growl, bringing himself up on his elbows and settling over her. "Juliana, you drive me to a need I cannot control. I planned to make this tender and slow."

She laughed and took hold of him, bringing him to her entrance, teasing both of them. "Ruari, will I ever tire of this?"

He whispered into her ear, "Take me inside you. Lead me home." She spread her legs and guided him until he took over, thrusting inside of her with a moan, stopping for a moment to make sure she'd accepted him with ease.

"More," she whispered.

He gave her what she wanted, picking up his rhythm until she matched him and they rocked the bed. When she was so slick he couldn't take it anymore, he said, "I cannot last much longer, love. Are you close?"

She spread her legs wide and answered him with a moan, her inner muscles contracting as she convulsed in pleasure, crying out his name. He careened off the edge with her.

They lay in each other's arms panting. He feathered her neck with tiny kisses simply because he was unable to speak.

He rolled onto his back and tucked her in close, sighing with pleasure.

"Ruari, do you know what saddens me?" she whispered, her hands playing with the coarse hairs on his chest.

"Hmmm?"

"That my sister never knew love the way it's supposed to be."

If it hadn't been for Juliana, he'd never have known either.

Juliana squeezed Ruari's hand as they approached Stonecroft Abbey. He helped her down from her horse and kissed her cheek.

"Are you happy, wife?"

"Verra."

"Good, because I've never been happier."

Ruari had taken on his new duties as Aedan's second, with Padraig as his assistant. They'd moved into the tower chamber, which the women of the clan had restored for them, and Ruari's mother had been moved to a chamber off the great hall. It would be easier for everyone to keep an eye on her, for the doorway had been widened.

Life was good.

Juliana glanced at her husband, the man she adored. She recalled the conversation he'd had with Aedan about how it had taken him a fire and a thunderstorm and a sweet lass to finally find himself, but as far as she was concerned Padraig had the right of it.

"You knew who you were when you told your brother Juliana was more important than being his second," he'd said. "You didn't need the fire to convince you of that."

She loved that he'd said that about her.

They'd spoken with the abbess, who'd confirmed Juliana did indeed have a niece. Moreover, she'd met her.

And so they'd come to Stonecroft Abbey on this cloudy day so that the abbess might bring them to Joan's daughter. Before they stepped inside the front door, Juliana had an odd compulsion to walk around the abbey to the back, so she tugged on Ruari's hand and led him that way without explaining why.

He didn't question what she was doing and she loved him for that, instead following her through a small garden and around a stone wall. The moment she stepped around the wall, she gasped. She lifted her gaze to his to see if he'd noticed.

He whispered, "'Tis the exact scene in your tapestry."

She laughed, raising her hands up to the sun that had just peeked out of the clouds, showering both of them with its warm rays. There, across the meadow full of lavender, stood her niece.

She was the missing piece in her needlework.

The lass smiled and began heading their way, so Juliana dropped her husband's hand and hurried to meet her.

Her hands were shaking when the lassie came to stand in front of her.

"I'm so glad you returned," Anora said, rushing in to

hug her. "We miss Sister Joan terribly. What will you do without her?"

Juliana noticed a bench off to the side, so she led the girl over to it while waving for Ruari to join them. "Have a seat, Anora."

The lass did as she was bid and Juliana could not help but stare at her.

She did indeed look like her dear sister Joan.

How had she missed it the first time? Their eyes were different, but her smile was Joan's, and so was her hair color.

"Do you remember how you told me you wished to know where you came from?"

Anora nodded.

"I'm here to tell you the truth. Sister Joan was your mother."

Anora's jaw dropped and she stood up, staring at her.

"You're my niece, and I'm here to take you home."

———◆———

Two moons later, Ruari paced in their tower room, wishing there was something he could do to help his wife. Juliana was hugging the basin while Anora mopped her forehead. "Just think how wonderful 'twill be when you hold your own bairn in your arms, Auntie."

Juliana groaned. "I know." She rinsed her mouth for the fourth time that day. He kissed her cheek and said, "I'll go find some fresh water and mayhap a wee bite of bread for you." He left the tower room in a hurry, wanting to get back to her as soon as possible. Although his heart had expanded so much he wondered how his chest could still contain it, he hated to see his wife suffer. He wished she'd get past the heaving stage.

Brin was on the floor not far from the door, playing with Heckie. He tossed a large stick across the room while the pup scampered after it, yipping at it as if it were alive.

"Heckie's getting big, Brin. You're doing a fine job

raising him."

The door to the courtyard opened with a bang and Neil strode inside, Aedan directly behind him. "Stop, Neil. 'Tis an order you'd be wise not to ignore."

Aedan's gaze shifted to Ruari, who'd already starting strolling toward the kitchens. "You'll wish to stay and hear this."

Ruari had no idea what was going on, but he heeded his brother, waiting to see what would happen next. Another man came in the door behind Aedan, but he stopped and waited for direction.

Neil stopped and spun on his heel, looking as if he intended to spar with Aedan, but Heckie ran over and tried to take a bite out of his ankle.

"Get the hell away from me, you wee bastard." Neil kicked at the pup and sent him flying across the hall.

Brin chased after him with a yelp as loud as the wee pup's.

"Neil, I'm warning you," Aedan said. "You'll stand there like a man and give us answers."

Neil put his hands on his hips, glaring first at Ruari, then at the man by the door, and finally at Aedan. "Fine. Do as you wish."

Aedan motioned to the visitor. "Ruari, this is one of the Munro guards who recently joined our clan. He felt he had some important information to share. Something that happened three years ago."

Ruari moved closer to ensure he'd hear what was said. "Go ahead."

The guard nodded to Aedan and Ruari, then said, "My lord and chief, 'twas three years ago when I noticed this man in front of me." He pointed to Neil, then continued, "He was talking with a beautiful dark-haired woman on horseback. She became so angry with him that she sent her horse into a fast gallop in a field only fit for a canter. He chased her, yelling at her to stop, but she didn't. She turned her head at one point to yell at him, but 'twas a bad time to turn. Her horse missed a log and fell on its foreleg, sending her flying. She landed poorly and broke her neck. I assisted him, getting her back on the horse so that he might return her to your castle because she was dead."

Aedan nodded to the man. "Many thanks to you. You are excused."

They watched as the man left, Ruari's insides in complete turmoil. What the hell did that mean?

Finally, after the door shut, Ruari turned to Neil and whispered, "So you were the reason she fled so quickly? It wasn't me?"

Neil's face moved through several emotions before he settled on sadness or possibly regret. "I saw her riding so I followed her. I wanted to know why the two of you had argued."

Aedan said, "And you upset her more. What did you say?"

"I told her Ruari was a fool. That she should have married someone like me. I didn't mean it—the marrying me part. I was alone. The woman I loved was a nun. I wanted…"

"You wanted my brother to be as miserable as you."

Neil didn't say anything, just glanced at Ruari. "I lied, and I shouldn't have. Not the first lie that's ever been told in our clan."

"But the consequences of your lie weigh so heavily on your conscience that you've done everything you can to cast blame on my brother."

Neil didn't say anything, just strode toward the door.

Aedan called out, "Neil! Wait."

Neil stopped but didn't turn around.

"You have ten minutes to gather your things. You're banished from Cameron land."

EPILOGUE

About seven months later

RUARI HELD HIS NEW SON in his arms, cradling his head and neck carefully as Juliana had taught him. He carried him over to his mother, seated by the big hearth with a plaid settled in her lap.

"Let me hold the wee one. He's such a handsome lad, is he not?" She held her arms up to the wee laddie.

"Aye, he is, Mama. I'll arrange him for you."

He set the babe in her lap, standing next to her to make sure she held him tightly enough. Juliana sat nearby, Anora next to her. Jennie and Aedan sat across from them in two chairs, while their three bairns had settled on the floor in front of the hearth.

"What shall we name him, Mama?" Ruari asked. He and Juliana had discussed possible names, but hadn't come up with any final decision, though they had a couple of favorites.

"I'm not sure. What think you, Aedan?"

"Dawy? Ludan?"

"Nay," Tara and Riley said in unison.

Jennie said, "What do you think, Juliana? You're his mother."

"I like Coll," she suggested.

He knew Coll to be one of her favorites, and he liked

it, too.

His mother said, "Nay, not quite right." She glanced down at the sleeping bairn, rubbing the palm of her hand carefully across his bald head. "Do you think his hair is red?"

"What about Ross? Or Mirren?" Brin asked.

They tossed about many names without settling on any one in particular, when finally his mother said rather loudly, "I have it!"

"What?" Jennie asked.

"Ruari, he looks like a Ruari."

The entire hall burst into laughter, but all Ruari could do was lean down and kiss his mother. "I think 'tis perfect, Mama. We'll call him Coll Ruari."

THE END

D EAR READER,

Thank you for reading! As always, reviews would be greatly appreciated. Sign up for my newsletter on my website at *www.keiramontclair.com*. I send newsletters out with each new release.

Another way to receive notices about my new releases is to follow me on BookBub. Click on the tab in the upper right-hand side of my profile page. You can also write a review on BookBub.

Keira Montclair

www.keiramontclair.com
www.facebook.com/KeiraMontclair
www.pinterest.com/KeiraMontclair

ABOUT THE AUTHOR

KEIRA MONTCLAIR IS THE PEN name of an author who lives in Florida with her husband. She loves to write fast-paced, emotional romance, especially with children as secondary characters in her stories.

She has worked as a registered nurse in pediatrics and recovery room nursing. Teaching is another of her loves, and she has taught both high school mathematics and practical nursing.

Now she loves to spend her time writing, but there isn't enough time to write everything she wants! Her Highlander Clan Grant series, comprising of eight standalone novels, is a reader favorite. Her third series, The Highland Clan, set twenty years after the Clan Grant series, focuses on the Grant/Ramsay descendants. She also has a contemporary series set in The Finger Lakes of Western New York.

Her latest series, The Band of Cousins, stems from The Highland Clan but is a stand-alone series.

Contact her through her website:
www.keiramontclair.com